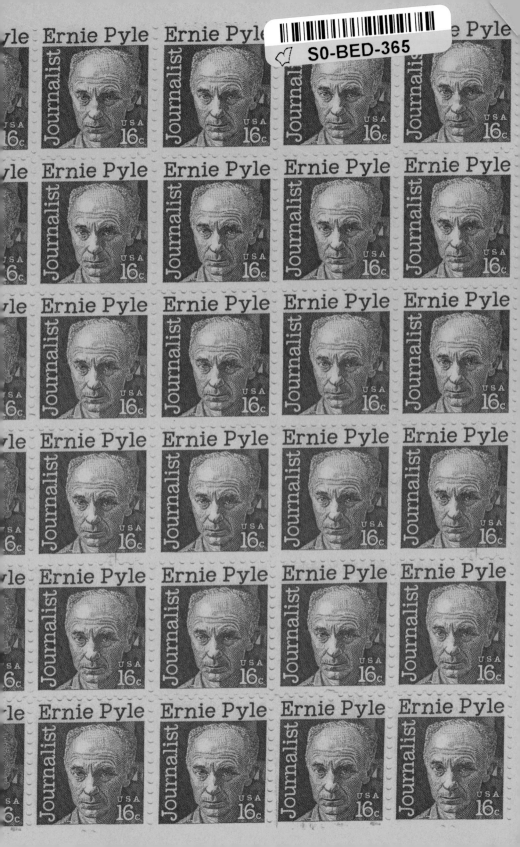

16 June, 2002

Happy Father's Day!

Love,
    Sarge

Ernie Pyle

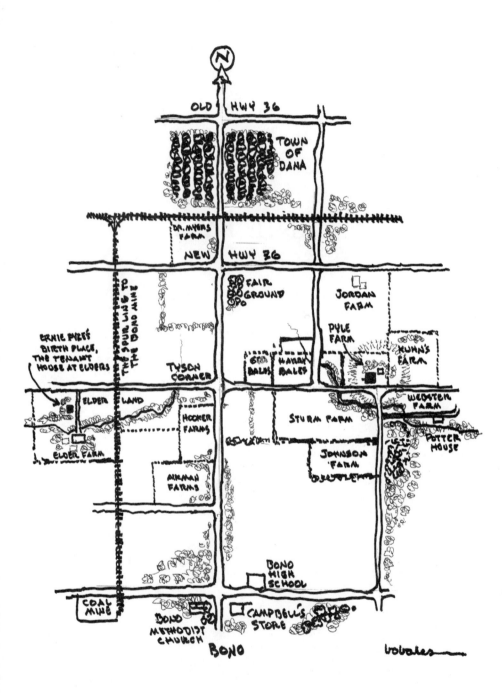

ERNIE PYLE

A HOOSIER CHILDHOOD

A Novel
Written and Illustrated by

Bob Bales

The Rivendell Book Factory · 2002

Limited Edition
ISBN 0-944353-10-X
Design by Jane Herlong
Production Design by Bill Segrest, Jr.

0 9 8 7 6 5 4 3 2 1 L

Contents

To the men and women who have served this country with great honor.

To Peggy, my beautiful wife, who encourages me in all my efforts.
To the future generations

Brett, Stuart, Tate, and Leeanna Bond
Parker and Nicholas Bryant
Rachel, Catherine, and Julie Burke
McKenzie Farrell
Sara and Andrew Frese
Susan and Andrew Goldstein
Gweena Mae Herd
Jane and Mallory Kraley
Evan and Hannah Mancer
Laura, Tyler, and Kyle Ogard
Gates and Houston Porter
I'Ans Reeder
Molly Rubell
Lindsey and Shelley Smith
Grace, Lexi, and Kit Turner
Joseph, Elizabeth, and Raines Welden

A special thanks to
Jim and Barbara Goforth and family
Gene Goforth and family
Mart, Sara, Andi, Andrew, and Chris Myers
And my "special" girls, Juanice, Ambur, and Michele
And, most of all, to my mother, Beatrice Bales, who was the one family
member Ernie always confided in throughout his life. She instilled in me
a love of art and history

Foreword

Ernie Pyle, the noted World War II journalist, was a writer who voiced his opinions objectively and fairly. He served his country by describing the everyday living conditions of the U.S. soldier overseas. He was the barometer of the soldier's world, and senior officers looked to his reports as a vital link in assessing troop readiness. America would eventually lose 292,131 men and women in the war effort, but it is because of writers like Ernie Pyle that we will never forget those who died for the freedom we now enjoy.

It is highly likely that someone close to you — your grandfather, your teacher, or your favorite librarian — has recommended that you read this novel. They have most likely recommended it to you because they believe a tale of growing up in the early 20th century will teach you what it means to be an American. They want you to understand, as they do, that history is more than just a bunch of dates. Understanding the ways of the past lays the foundation on which you and your friends are going to build the future.

Ernie Pyle was known as the "Hoosier Vagabond" and later as the "Roving Reporter." He set out during the Great Depression, on a $5-a-day budget, with the assignment of writing about ordinary people. He could write an interesting story about almost any subject that came along. His weekly newspaper columns suggested that just because something looks one way, it could, in fact, have another side altogether. You just have to look carefully, Pyle believed, and when you do you will be surprised at what you find.

Pyle's style was strictly "country," with few fancy words or phrases. He wrote the way he talked. As his close friend, Paige Cavanaugh, once said, "Ernie . . . had great humor in him and a deep interest in unimportant people." Ernie Pyle was a man who wanted to inspire common men and women to act heroically, to encourage every individual to strive to make a difference. Pyle would go on to become the voice of the front lines in WWII, his daily columns appearing in over 500 newspapers across America.

On December 7, 1941, the Japanese bombed the American naval base at Pearl Harbor in Hawaii. America entered World War II. A few years ago, friends of mine, Richard & Wanda Stanberry, visited the Punch Bowl Cemetery, nestled high above Honolulu in the crater of an extinct volcano. In this ethereal, almost spooky setting, the tour guide stopped the group as they were following a path among the countless grave markers. "Here is where Ernie Pyle lies buried among his combat buddies," he announced.

From the very back of the group an American teenager whined, "Who in the world is Ernie Pyle?" She might as well have been saying, "I want to get back to the beach to get some more sun." Such casual disrespect, standing among the graves of the men and women who had died in the bombing, deeply offended my friends. It's not that she didn't know who Ernie Pyle was, *it's that she didn't seem to care.*

It is vitally important that each of you, my young readers, remember those who have come before you and the lessons they have taught. It is my sincere hope that this story about Ernie Pyle will set you on a path of discovery to learn more about the writings of other storytellers and chroniclers who have help to shape our nation's history.

Having been raised with the Pyle family and having shared the same graveled road, I share their family history and know the stories that have endured in our close-knit farm community. I first heard about Ernie's growing-up years from Maria and Will Pyle, and then later from my parents, Bill and Beatrice Bales, and from my grandmother, Mary Bales, known by everyone, including Ernie, as Aunt Mary. Ernie's parents were always "Aunt Maria" and "Uncle Will" to my brother Jack and me. We were always treated like their own.

But as time slips by, the facts of the matter slip a little also. This is my effort to set the record straight, before we forget, and provide a snapshot of what farm life was like in the Midwest at the beginning of last century. I want to tell you where Ernie Pyle, "the voice of the soldier," came from and how I believe his humble background created the kind of writer who would so accurately capture the American spirit.

I hope if you like it you will recommend this slice of history to someone you know.

Blest Indiana! In whose soil
Men seek the sure rewards of toil,
And honest poverty and worth
Find here the best retreat on earth ...

John Finley

Chapter 1

_____

The Good Doctor Makes a House Call

"When did she have her first labor pains, Lambert?" asked the doctor politely in his usual professional manner.

"Yesterday afternoon, as best we can tell," replied Lambert Taylor. "She's had so many pains over the past few days, we just don't know for sure."

It was shortly after 5 a.m. on August 3, 1900, when Doc Keys answered the knock at his back door to find Taylor, nervous and concerned, asking to come in. Taylor had just driven his buggy three miles to Dana, the small town at the heart of this Indiana farming community. Taylor's daughter, Maria Pyle, was going to have a baby and the anxious grandfather-to-be had come to fetch the doctor.

Mr. Taylor was a quiet man, a farmer of solid Midwestern stock who rarely showed emotion. Doc Keys could plainly tell he was upset.

"You know how much she means to me, Doc. Do you reckon she'll have any trouble because of her age," he asked.

Maria was now 30 years old and many people believed a

woman of her years shouldn't be having a baby. There had been a lot of talk around the county about Maria and Will Pyle getting married so late in life. Trying to raise a family at such an age was just not the normal flow of things in this close-knit farming community.

"Some of the womenfolk say this might be a breech birth, Doc. Any chance of that?"

Doc Keys offered Taylor another cup of coffee and then took a long sip from his own cup, the old mustache cup his father, Dr. Cuthbert Keys, had given him when he had first learned to shave. The Taylors and the Keys had always been good neighbors so Doc Keys felt comfortable being direct.

"Lambert, a breech birth can happen to any expectant mother of any age. It does happen sometimes, but rarely." There was compassion and warmth in Doc Keys' voice, a quality that seemed to come easily to him. "I don't want you to fret about it. I have instruments to care for most any emergency."

"I know you do, Doc, it's just . . . Maria shouldn't be having a baby at her age, that's all," sighed Taylor. He put down his empty cup and adjusted his suspenders. Doc had seen the same before with other farmers. He knew that Taylor was just overly anxious and nervous about his little girl, and that in spite of his grumpiness he was soon going to be the proudest man in the county. A grandchild would be born and all worry would fade away.

Doc Keys excused himself to prepare for the trip to Will and Maria Pyle's. As he was leaving the kitchen, he saw Taylor reach into his hip pocket and pull out a small Bible. Doc understood that Taylor's story was the story of most of the hard-working farmers in the county — soiled, in patched and faded work clothes, this scrappy Midwesterner would forever remain steadfast in his convictions and fierce in his loyalties.

There is a certain rhythm to life in a farming community, and the little town of Dana was slowly awakening beneath a purplish-pink summer sunrise. The milkman from Norton's dairy was just now making his rounds. The clip-clop of horses' hooves echoed off the brick streets crisscrossing the town. The iceman, too, was making deliveries, hurrying to beat the August heat that was sure to come later in the day. For the most part, however, the town would remain quiet and still until mid-morning.

Dana was in the heart of Indiana farm country in the early 1900s, and, because of the high productivity of the area farms, the grain elevator, just next door to the railroad depot, would become a hubbub of activity later in the day. If you were a farmer, this was the best place in town to take a break and catch up on the community gossip. The boys at the grain elevator referred to Lambert Taylor as "the homeliest man in the township." It was all in good-natured fun, of course, because Taylor was such a good man and people respected him so. You could bet they'd be talking about his new grandchild before too long.

Underneath the pitched roof of the railroad depot was a large sign reading "Dana." Charlie Peters, the telegrapher, was able to send messages all over the country from behind his desk. Mr. Bechtel provided the local farmers with a dray service. He had a big Percheron horse to pull his iron-wheeled wagon. The wheels of most commercial wagons in Dana were rimmed with iron and what a noise they would make as they came rolling through town each day. To keep the iron from sloughing off in hot weather, the owners would park their wagons in a shallow pool of water at the end of a workday. The wooden wheels would swell up and the rims would remain tight for a few days.

When a wagonload of grain arrived at the elevator, it was first weighed on the flat farm scales. The horses would then pull the heavy load up a ramp to the dumping station. The tailgate was removed, and the grain would spill through the trap door into a dusty and dark cellar of pulleys, belts, wheels and bins. The great clamor and hum of all this machinery and activity often spooked the horses. They would have to be coaxed up the ramp a second time, wild-eyed and shaking, to wait for the wagon to be emptied.

Standing next to the railroad tracks, the grain elevator allowed the wheat, oats, and corn to be loaded easily on to a cross-country train by siphoning off large quantities through shunting troughs. Once a boxcar was loaded, its heavy car doors were slammed and bolted shut, ready for transport to Decatur.

Lambert Taylor had come from a large family. His father had been born in Delaware in 1794, and was one of the early pioneers in Vermillion County, Indiana. Maria Pyle, who was at this very moment having his grandchild, was his youngest daughter, his "baby" as he often referred to her. She was born outside of Tuscola, Illinois, at Cherry Point in 1870, the youngest of the three children. When Taylor's wife, Lucinda, died of consumption, what we now know as tuberculosis, he and his children moved back to Indiana to be near the Taylor kinfolk.

Taylor had been a very strict father and had worked his children hard, but he loved them dearly. His daughters had always been considered the old maids of the neighborhood and the conventional wisdom in the county had it that Mary and Maria were so overly protected that neither would ever catch a man — let alone produce a grandchild!

"I'll get right down there to the Elder place, Lambert," replied the doctor matter-of-factly. "Shouldn't take much over an hour; I just had Belle re-shod at Fulwider's last week. These gravel roads are hard on horses, you know."

"Should I come along?" asked Taylor sheepishly.

Doc Keys understood that Taylor really didn't want to

return to the Pyle household. Birthing was not a place for men. "Oh, I reckon not, Lambert. Is there a woman with her?"

"Her sister Mary went over there yesterday. Stayed all night."

"Has Mary been a midwife before?"

"No, but she's real good with cows and livestock. She can handle most anything in that respect; I don't know how she'll do with her own sister though." Taylor was only able to manage a weak smile. "Maria's had a long and difficult pregnancy, Doc. Been ill a lot. Put on a lot of weight, too. Her first, you know . . . " His voice trailed off.

Doc Keys sought to reassure Taylor. "Between Mary and me and the Lord, we'll do our best to deliver you an heir, Lambert," he said. "I promise you that."

Doc Keys, in coat and tie, was just a small-town, country doctor delivering babies and tending to the sick. He was the last, best hope for a family facing an illness or trauma. He oftentimes had to endure great sacrifice to minister to the sick around the county. When the call came, the complications and the circumstances of an illness or accident could never be fully appreciated until he got to the patient's home. On countless occasions, his responsibilities as well as his commitment to the healing arts would unexpectedly take him away from his own family for days at a time.

Maybe Taylor would pay him $5.00, maybe Taylor would pay him $2.00, or maybe Taylor would trade it out in eggs and butter. "But whatever may come," thought Doc Keys, as he climbed into his buggy, "it just wouldn't be right to send Taylor a bill for bringing a youngster into the world." Doc Keys tossed his black leather medical bag on the floorboard and headed out of town.

Chapter 2

Ernest Taylor Pyle

"Giddyup," commanded Doc Keys, approaching Old Toronto corner, about a mile and a half south of Dana. He snapped the reins with more authority than he had intended and then, correcting himself, whispered in softer tones to Belle, his faithful buggy mare, "Come on, girl, we've got a baby to deliver down here in Sam Elder's woods."

Three miles of gravel road, which ultimately lead to the larger town of Bono, Indiana, was lined with Osage orange hedgerows and an occasional large hackberry, elm, maple or cottonwood tree. It was rich farmland, as black as coalies' boots the local farmers would say. The apple orchard now covering 10 acres on the east side of the road at the Corner was planted right after the Civil War. The Hookers, the Elders, and the Rhoades owned most of the land at this active crossroad.

Just prior to the Civil War, the Elders had obtained their land grant. They put down roots and, now, three generations later, Sam Elder was running the family farm. Sam had needed help, so Will Pyle and his new bride, Maria Taylor Pyle, had agreed to move into the little tenant house in Elder's woods, a stretch of farmland and timber running almost a mile west of Tyson Corner. Sam Elder's tenant house was extremely uncomfortable, but others had survived the same experience and it was this humble dwelling that Doc Keys was now headed towards to deliver Maria Pyle's baby.

Doc Keys had traveled many a muddy back road in Vermillion County over the years, taking care of the sick and the dying as well as delivering babies. "Someone had to care for these good country folks," he chuckled to himself, "and I guess God put the touch on me."

Practicing medicine hadn't been easy since many of his patients were simple folk who had their own remedies. He smiled as he thought back on the many years it had taken him to coax these good people away from their cow-manure poultices (for boils), slippery elm bark elixirs (for diarrhea), and turpentine draughts (for tapeworms). Some of these treatments worked, of course, but unsanitary conditions and infection were persistent problems that had to be addressed responsibly by members of the modern medical profession. That was his job and his calling.

Dr. O.M. Keys was a household name in Helt Township, Vermillion County, Indiana. Doc Keys had met everyone in the countryside by practicing medicine with his father from their small office on Main Street in Dana. His father had died in 1885, leaving a very active practice for him to handle alone. Never one to sit idle, Doc Keys had also taught school and had been a trustee of Helt Township. Prospects were bright in the early 1900s, with the extremely productive farms on the outskirts of Dana now being served by the new railroad.

"And soon my son Paul is going to be practicing with me," he said aloud to Belle, interrupting his thoughts, "so maybe I'll get some rest." Doc Keys often caught himself talking to himself these days. Especially when he was on the road. He had resigned himself to the fact that he was no longer a spring chicken. He'd be 46 in three more days. "Darn near worn to the cob," he said aloud. Belle shook her head violently, trying to rid herself of a big horsefly that had latched onto her flank.

Usually there were quite a few buggies on the road at this time of the morning, but because of the muddy roadway it was now quiet. He had earlier passed the fairgrounds south of town and had been surprised to see that they were afloat with water. The smell of the stalls and horse barns had drifted across the humid countryside to greet him. Several large limbs had been blown off the tall maple trees, which lined the fair park, and some of the tasseled corn crop was lying flat from the strong winds of the night's thunderstorm. It must've been some gulley washer, Doc Keys thought.

Instinctively, Doc Keys pulled on the right reins as his four wheeler cut around the corner and headed due west toward the Illinois State line. The Randalls, the Elders, the Holberts, and the Bells lived out there, straight ahead. Although the narrow roadbed had been patched with gravel, it was now laced with deep ruts and wide pools of water.

The creek that drained the big swamp on the north side of the road was flooding over the little plank bridge anchored there in a clump of sturdy willow trees. Belle was nervous about walking through the swirling brown water, which was up to her knees. Calmly Doc urged her on, and she responded faithfully. Belle and the good doctor had been through floods, windstorms, and snow squalls together on many a back road.

It was a good mile west to the gate that led into Sam Elder's place. "About half a mile to go," thought Doc Keys. They met one buggy on the road west; it was Charlie Holbert on his way to town to fetch some cornmeal from Tom Clark at the main grocery store.

He waived at Doc Keys and then yelled, "Somebody sick down here in the woods?"

"Maria Pyle's in labor. Gotta hurry!" Doc Keys replied.

Their buggies passed in a swirl of harness, mud, and horseflesh.

The gate was just ahead now. Slowly, he pulled Belle off to the south side of the road into a muddy trail that led south through the woods. He got out to open the gate to the pasture. The August sun was hot, even at this early hour, and the humidity was already stifling. Doc Keys and Belle were both switching and swatting flies. He patted the mare gently on her rump as he got back in the buggy after closing the gate.

The humidity boiled up from the damp pasture as Doc Keys headed south along the fence toward the tenant house on Sam Elder's farm. He could see the main house sitting back through the oak and hickory trees that shaded the rolling pastureland. Sam Elder's white, two-story house sat on a knoll just across the creek that ran though the woods. Off to his right he could see the little three-room tenant house, unpainted and nestled safely in a clump of scrub maples and wild rose bushes.

"What a start for this poor little family," Doc Keys thought to himself. "Not a chance in the world that the child will ever amount to much. He's starting with nothing, and he'll probably end with nothing." But, then, after a few more moments, he reflected that this rich farmland produced a strong strain of men. The success of the community was proof of that. No one ever went hungry and no one walked away from hard work. "Someday this area will be on the map," he thought, "even if no one ever remembers the name of Dr. O.M. Keys."

Doc Keys pulled slightly on the rein. Belle came to a slow walk and headed toward the house. He was almost there now. A thought flashed through his mind, and he began to panic, "What if it is a breech birth and I lost both of them? After all, old Lambert laid it all on me."

He had only last month called on a young farm girl who died shortly after childbirth. She had hemorrhaged badly despite all of the techniques he had tried. She just kept bleeding. He was helpless. The expectant father was so crushed by it all that he said he wanted to die, too. Doc Keys had spoken to him softly about how God gives and takes away and about how we are not to question these things.

Despite the 80-degree heat and the sweat trickling down his neck, his palms felt cool. For a brief moment, he was scared. "I'm out here alone. I have no help!" He then took a deep breath, "Dear God, you have helped me before. If it is your will, let this mother and baby have a normal birth . . . ." Doc Keys was a man of faith who believed in the power of prayer to calm the family, strengthen the patient, and affirm life. Prayer was an essential element in his practice of medicine.

Doc Keys reined Belle to a quick stop in the front of the little tenant house, as a redheaded woodpecker flashed across the path in front of him. The woods were steaming hot and the sounds of the birds and the cicadas made this an amphitheater of hurried tension.

With black satchel in hand, he swung easily out of the buggy and left Belle under a shade tree.

He was relieved when Mary Taylor greeted him at the door, "Thank God you've made it, Dr. Keys! Maria has been in labor for so long I don't know what to do." He removed his hat as he stepped inside and placed it upon a cane bottom chair near the stove.

"I got the message early this morning, Mary, and I came right down," replied Doc Keys, who scanned the room to see the best arrangement he could set up. He was wearing a wrinkled gray suit. The white shirt had been clean and starched when he left the stable behind his house well over an hour ago, but now the shirt was drenched with sweat. His thin black tie was as limp as a noodle. He appeared to be a man of great confidence, but only he knew how hard he had worked to develop that confidence — through faith, education, and experience.

After a preliminary examination, Doc Keys leaned over Maria and gently brushed back the red hair from her forehead. "You've suffered long enough, Maria. It shouldn't be too long now. Mary, lets get Maria more comfortable." He instructed Mary to help him turn her crosswise on the bed so he could have some room to work.

"When did she go into labor?" asked Doc Keys as he felt Maria's pulse.

"Around supper time last night. The first ones didn't last long. I thought they would go away and that she would be all right till morning. Will sat up with her all night through the storm. He was afraid that the wind would blow a tree down on the house."

"Oh, doctor," whimpered Maria, "the pains are coming faster now." She was positioned on her back with her knees drawn up. "I can't push any harder, it hurts too much."

Doc Keys went to the basin and hurriedly washed his hands, returning quickly with sleeves rolled up above his elbows, medical kit in hand.

"Now, you'll have to help me," he instructed Mary.

The tiny, confined space in the little shack was sticky hot, as humid as sorghum molasses. Maria Pyle was intermittently racked with pain. Black houseflies were laced along the ceiling.

Doc Keys reckoned that Maria Pyle must have been in labor at least 15 hours. The pains were coming in rapid succession now and the dilation was obvious. "Not much longer now," and then, in a brief moment of silence, Dr. Keys, thanked God. The baby was headfirst! It wasn't going to be a breech birth after all!!

"The baby is coming along nicely now," Doc reassured his patient with a calming enthusiasm. Maria Pyle was about to give forth new life, a redheaded spark of the future generation. Doctor Keys, by nature a reserved and methodical man, finally shouted, "It's a boy, it's a boy!" And he held up a new baby as if all the world was there in witness.

"Oh, Maria, it's a precious little boy," said Mary. "He has lots of red hair just like you."

"Mary, dear," said Maria, still very weak and wet with perspiration, but beaming like a rainbow, "we're going to call him Ernest Taylor Pyle." One day, she thought, like every new mother before her, the whole world will know his name.

Chapter 3

―――

Sam Elder's Place

The blackberries had come in a few weeks ago, in early July. Will had picked two large buckets for canning and he now topped two heavy slices of fresh baked bread, one for him and one for Mary, his sister-in-law, with the butter and fresh blackberry jam that Maria, his wife, had put up just last week. Mary would be moving in to help Maria with the baby. They were very close even for sisters. Will looked across the breakfast table at Mary; he realized how happy he was going to be to have her helping out for a few months . . . even if it did mean close quarters.

He always went to work at sun-up and quit at sundown; he was relieved when Mary had kicked him out of the house at 5 a.m. after he had had his breakfast of coffee, two fried eggs, and some sowbelly fried in heavy grease. Even though his wife was soon going to have a baby, Will was a hard-working man and the farm chores had to come first. He was happy to leave Maria in the care of her sister, and was confident that her father, Lambert Taylor, was well on his way to getting Doc Keys from Dana.

A man who has no land in a farming community often

becomes a hired hand, taking almost any job that comes his way. Opportunities were mighty slim, and a hired hand was little more than a "gopher." There was always something to be done and the hired hand had to "go fer" this and "go fer" that. Clean out the chicken house, muck the horse stalls, move the pig feeding lot, tend to the cows. And these chores would come after the hired hand had completed the heavier jobs assigned earlier in the day!

Farm men left the birthing experience to the women. Will couldn't have done anything anyhow and besides, farm hands are supposed to be in the fields, not hanging around the house. Sam Elder didn't take a shine to shirking duties. Will started the day by herding the six cows into the back barn and feeding them and the eight horses Mr. Elder kept to work his land. After the pigs were slopped with a mixture of soaked oats and corn, it was time to start the milking. The rain last night had left the cows standing knee-deep in barnyard mud, so milking them was going to be a dirty mess. The cows were of a nasty disposition due to the biting flies and the sultry heat.

Samuel Elder was the third generation to own the land that Will Pyle now worked. Elder lived with his wife and his mother in a dwelling built in 1881, an impressive house for the time, set back in the woods about a quarter-mile off the main road. Sam made sure there were horses and buggies for the ladies. Elder was among the few landowners in the township who had acquired or inherited large tracts of rich farm land, woodlands, herds of cattle, horses, and sheep through earlier land grants or perhaps, it was rumored, through political shenanigans. The more these big landowners acquired, the hungrier they seemed for more.

Maria, even though she was pregnant, had helped Mrs. Elder as much as she could. Maria felt a strong compassion for the Elder family because they didn't have many friends and were demanding neighbors. The Elders seldom went to town and didn't seem interested in associating with other farmers and townsfolk. When Elder shot and injured one of a neighbor's dog, his reputation was sealed . . . at least as far as the children were concerned.

There a was a dirt road that led back to the house, crossing a little creek and winding its way through a green canopy of hickory and oak trees. It was beautiful country; it was a bountiful land. As a hired hand much was expected of Will Pyle. Elder had had other hired hands, but they hadn't stayed around long. Many of them had left before the harvest started in order to avoid the long days and heavy physical work. It took the stamina of a mule to satisfy Sam Elder.

After cleaning up the barn and getting the buckets of milk delivered to the back porch of the Elder home, Will picked up the one bucket of milk he was promised each day. He headed across the muddy creek at the foot log and made his way through the woods to his house. He left the milk on the little kitchen table for Mary and went over to the bedside of his wife to give her some words of encouragement. She was a farm girl and knew that his job was in the fields, not midwifery, she told him.

Will said a silent prayer and kissed his wife. Mary was handling the situation admirably even though she would have been much happier had Doc Keys already arrived. It was just past 6:45 a.m. when Will left the tenant house for the second time that morning. He had work to do along the eastern fencerow just below the barn now. Working along the fence, digging out blackberry vines with a mattock, was easier than most other chores and it offered him a good time to take his mind off his pregnant wife and dream about the future.

When Will Pyle and Maria Taylor married, it was hardly an earth-shaking social event. They got married the first day in

November 1899 and held the ceremony at the Bono Methodist Church, the only church they had ever known. Lambert Taylor was proud to be giving away his youngest in marriage at long last. After all, his three children had grown up and all were still living with him; it was about time one of them married! He liked Will Pyle, who came from a good family, but he was a bit concerned that Will didn't seem to have any future or trade. Taylor knew it would be hard going for the young couple, but at least there would be another man in the family when help was needed, and Will Pyle was a decent hard-working man.

Will Pyle came from the old Pyle farm over in the woods about two miles northeast of the Taylor place. His father, Samuel Pyle, had purchased the farm outright at the turn of the Civil War and brought his new bride, Nancy Hammond, there to live and raise a family. It was a 200-acre farm, mostly timberland with some good soil for crops. It was a challenging task to clean out the underbrush and stumps to make it suitable for farming. Gradually, however, Samuel Pyle scraped out a living and was able to raise his five children Mattie, Will, Quince, Clarence, and Frances in the meantime.

When it was time for Will to move out into the world, all he had to recommend his prospects was 40 acres of hardscrabble and timber. Having labored on a farm all of his life, from the time he was old enough to carry a milk bucket, he had the unbounded confidence he would succeed. One Sunday afternoon at the little brick church just a half-mile east of the Taylor place Will attended a neighborhood picnic. Several of his friends were there. Although he knew of the Taylor sisters, he had never met them before. They were attending the picnic with their stern and dominating father, Lambert Taylor. The families brought several covered dishes and cakes and pies. During the course of the afternoon, he met Maria Taylor.

Although she was not considered a beauty, she had lovely red hair that blew in the wind. Will took an immediate fancy to her and finally got up the nerve to talk with her.

"I live over at the Pyle place in the woods," he volunteered bashfully. "I work all week, but usually have Sundays off."

Maria Taylor was never one to be short of words, so she threw back her red hair and said, "Why don't you come by our place next Sunday?" This was the start of a lifelong romance, which never ended.

Will was soon working as a hired hand way over on the other side of the Wabash River, some eight miles to the east. When he was courting Maria, every Sunday he would drive a buggy six miles to the river, row a boat across, and then ride a bicycle ten miles to her house. At midnight he reversed the process. Maria figured he either loved her, or was foolish enough to need someone to look after him, so she married him.

Walking the Elder fence line, Will thought about how lucky he was and realized that probably at this very minute his wife was having his baby.

Will had been working all morning digging out a patch of wild blackberries that had overgrown Elder's fence rail. It was awfully hot and muggy out in the boiling sun. He had sweated clear through his dark blue cotton shirt and his straw hat was wet all around the band. The rain last night had turned the entire woodlands into a steam room. He knew by the sun that it was getting close to noon, and he could see the empty buggy of Dr. Keys parked under the maple tree in front of the house. With anxious steps he hurried north across the creek, then another 200 yards through the woods to the tenant house. Will Pyle was small and wiry, but he was carrying the maddox ax across his thin shoulders like a man twice his size. He burst through the front door of his little home and saw the bundle of new life in his wife's arms. With a pleasant smile and a twinkle in his blue eyes, there was nothing he could say. He went to his wife's side and hugged her.

Sam Elder had hired Will to work for one year at $12 a month, which included living in the tenant house, and free milk and eggs. Being a tenant farmer was no joy, but Will was determined to stick it out and was glad to have had a job when he found out Maria was pregnant. He was even happier now as he took his first look at his new baby boy.

"He looks just like you, Maria," crowed Will as he was handed his new son. The baby had been thoroughly washed and checked over by Dr. Keys. Mary Taylor had wrapped the tiny tot in the swaddling clothes some of the neighbor women had given as gifts at the baby shower held at Lou Lockridge's home just east of the Taylor place.

"I'll get the scales from the kitchen," said Will before Dr. Keys had uttered even the first word about weighing the baby.

Will held the hanging scales by the strap at the top while Dr. Keys placed the newborn wrapped in a clean pillowcase into the tray.

"Hold still, Will, so we can read the scales," said Mary, as persnickety as ever.

"Let me check that scale again, Will," replied the doctor. "Take off a half-pound for the wrapping," he turned the face of the scale towards the window where he could see it better, "and he'll come in about six and one-half pounds. I know how proud your father will be Maria, to know that he finally is a grandfather."

There was much hugging and kissing and crying in the little tenant house down in Sam Elder's woods that noon on August 3, 1900.

"I'd better be heading back to town now. I think it's going to rain again this afternoon. It's just too hot and humid," grinned the doctor as he put on his coat and closed up his little black medical bag.

"Now, before you go, Dr. Keys, you let Will give your horse some feed and water while I set something out for dinner." Mary was now happy to have the tension relieved and was taking charge. "I've got a chicken already fried, some fresh baked bread and we have some ripe tomatoes out of the garden. I baked a blackberry pie for Will last night, but I don't think it is any good. I'm not used to this old wood stove," Mary half-apologized.

"Really, Mary, I have to get back and besides, I'm too worn out to enjoy such a fine dinner. You and Will go ahead and eat and I'll feed Belle when we get back to town. It's awfully hot and she might get sick on a belly full of oats in this heat."

As Doc Keys was leaving through the gate at the Elder place, he was thinking about how much he missed his father and how he wished that his father were alive to be part of this occasion. He always loved bringing life into the world and he thought so much of the Taylor girls. He was sure that his father, more optimistic and encouraging than Teddy Roosevelt himself, would have said that without a doubt this young boy would amount to something in spite of his humble beginnings.

Chapter 4

New Life at the Mound

Will and Maria Pyle had discussed moving out of the tenant shack long before the baby had arrived. The Elder place was simply a port in a storm, not where they would put down roots. When Maria learned she was pregnant, she and Will made plans to move several months after the baby was born; Will was determined to honor his commitment to Sam Elder by working through the fall harvest until the corn had been shucked and in the crib. Their plan was to move in with Maria's father, Lambert Taylor, in early November 1900. Taylor, of course, would be over-joyed to have his daughter back home with him, especially since he would have the chance to be with his only grandson most of the winter.

When Taylor purchased his farm, known as the Mound, in 1895, he had 78 acres with a log barn and a four-room house with a small attic. The log barn was built before the Civil War from heavy black walnut logs cut from the surrounding mixed hardwood forests. Clearing the land of stumps and brush was a constant chore. There was a lot of timber throughout the community, and much time was spent clearing some of the land for crops. Gradually, Mr. Taylor acquired a sizable collection of horses and cows and a lean-to on the backside of the barn for milking. Then he added some sheep to his barnyard.

The Mound, as the Taylor place has always been referred to, is a curious bulge of earth, perhaps a quarter of a mile in diameter, rising probably 100 feet above the surrounding terrain. Some have said it was an old Indian burial mound, while others referred to it as yet another geological oddity, for just a half mile north on the Will Jordan farm is a similar mound. The soil around the Mound is mostly clay, unlike the rich, black land that lies directly to the west.

Shortly after moving to the Mound, Taylor landed a contract to furnish gravel from the Mound for the dirt roadways in Helt Township. The county and state agreed to pay him 25 cents a yard for the gravel. This operation got underway in 1896 and the excavation of hundreds of loads of gravel from the Mound left a gaping hole in the west side. The men who hauled the gravel made $1.00 a day providing that they furnished their own wagon and a team of horses.

The Mound yielded a much-needed, valuable commodity — gravel — as this was farmland and gravel beds were nowhere in sight. Graveling the roads had been a major concern of highway commissioner William Bales, and there was plenty of gravel right there under Lambert Taylor's nose. This natural gravel pit was discovered when the roadways were surveyed in square mile patterns. One such road started at the Oll Staats farm to the east and ran straight west to the Illinois line, a distance of five miles.

Another road came up from the south and made a T-junction at the Mound. Originally, this road went all the way through to the north, but Mr. Taylor somehow got this range line closed and later absorbed this roadway into his farm. Throughout the history of this part of Indiana, there has been constant references to the Mound, as it was a subject of some controversy. Was it a scared Indian burial ground?

Will Pyle defied expectations by staying on at Sam Elder's place for the full harvest, never complaining. Elder was a short man, red cheeks, shiny glasses, clean overalls, and gumboots. He hired people and they seldom stayed long. Sam Elder had run off many hired hands before the harvest because he worked them so hard in the summer months. Throughout the grueling work and physical labor, the dream of working his own place, building his own sheds, remodeling his own house, and caring for his own livestock kept him going.

Will had now completed all of the heavy farm work for Elder. He had given him notice. It had been a mild fall with winter just around the corner. Now that he was a father, Will Pyle looked forward to settling in with his father-in-law, Mr. Taylor, at the Mound before the snow flew.

He and Maria were now moving out. Sam Elder was standing behind the wagon brought over by Mr. Taylor. The Pyle family was loading up right in front of the tenant house. "What will I do without you, Will? Who's going to care for the livestock, the chickens, and the chores?" Sam Elder pleaded.

Will continued loading, saying nothing.

Sam Elder watched all of this activity and decided he must make one last plea. He swallowed his pride and said, "Are you sure you want to pull out of here, Will, with that new baby, and move back to the Mound? I sure could use you."

"Mr. Elder, there comes a time when a man has to move on, and I want to get my own place and do my own work . . . "

"Will, you will never be anything but a hired hand. Your people depend on people like me to give you a job no matter where you go," Sam elder sneered. "I tell you what, I'll even raise your pay to $14 per month."

Will just smiled and shook his head and threw the last of their belongings on the wagon. "Well, Mr. Elder, we're loaded up. It's time for us to get moving," replied the gentle little man.

"Here, Will," said Elder as he handed him his pay for the last month, $12 in cash. "I didn't pay you right away. I figured you'd use it up before you packed up to move."

"Thanks Mr. Elder, I do need the money."

"Just a minute, Will, my policy is to check the inside of the house before you go. I do it for all my tenants. Sometimes people carry off things that aren't theirs, like a bucket or broom or a chair. These things cost money, you know."

"I understand. I think you'll find everything is okay, but I understand your wantin' to check it out. You know, we wouldn't take anything that wasn't ours, Mr. Elder."

"Well, I reckon not, Will, but a man in my position can never be too sure." Will Pyle watched as Sam Elder went into the little house. Will could hardly believe Elder was just there, standing right in front of him, almost accusing him of thievery!

Elder came out of the cabin, satisfied. Maria began walking toward the buggy. "Will, fix me a place to sit in the wagon bed, so I can keep little Ernest warm. It feels like snow and ice might not be too long off." Elder finally said, "We're going to miss you and Will, Maria. You are the best working couple we've ever had here on the farm."

"Thank you. We've got a new baby, Sam. We want the best for him. I'm sure you understand."

"He'll make a good farm hand one day, Maria."

"He's going to make his own place one day, Sam," replied Maria Pyle, turning to take a last look at the little tenant house where her first and only child was born. "We're going to church Sunday to count our blessings," said Maria as she and Will and little Ernest set out towards their new life.

The winter of 1901 was a mild one, which was altogether fortunate because the living arrangements of the tiny four-room house behind the Mound on the north slope were stretched to their limits. The Taylor household, Lambert and his only son, John, and his unmarried daughter, Mary, had now increased by three, Will, Maria, and little Ernest. As any doting mother would do, Maria Pyle immediately staked out her claim on a bedroom for the baby. That cold little northwest corner of the tiny homestead from that time on was known as "Ernie's room."

Lambert Taylor was a practical man of vision. They would not last long as a close and loving family in such close quarters. Why not just move the house and start all over again? Add more space and improve their living conditions at the same time? For a moment, Taylor considered moving it on the snow during the dead of winter, but when he realized they could not vacate the house that long and survive, he elected to wait for the spring of 1901 to put his plan into action.

On a cold blustery day in late March 1901, Mr. Theopolus Ammerman came by to talk to Taylor. Mr. Ammerman was an expert at moving buildings. Taylor was happy that his son-in-law, Will Pyle, was such a handyman with tools. His reputation in the county was that he could build anything, so he and Mr. Ammerman were asked to visualize the whole procedure. Will and Mr. Ammerman carefully stepped off the area, measured the house, crawled under it, and finally came to the conclusion that it could be moved on log rollers. The plan was that Will Pyle was to fetch some dozen logs about 8 to 12 inches in diameter, and preferably oak so they wouldn't split. Mr. Taylor visited his neighbors and got 18 head of horses committed for the job. The move would require extra singletrees, doubletrees, plus a lot of chains to properly execute the plan.

Early in the morning of April 16, 1901, Dr. John Sturm, Harry Bales, Frank Bales, William Bales, Robert Webster, Jim Ingram, and Frank Kuhns arrived at the Taylor house with an assortment of workhorses and equipment and set right to work. Mr. Taylor had picked out an ideal site for the house, but before they reached it, the rollers started breaking apart, some of the chains broke, and the horses got out of control. The solution was to leave the house where it rested.

Mary, Maria, and little Ernest had moved into the log barn to set up housekeeping a few days before the move. It was cozy, but cold. The heavy walnut logs kept out the wind, and the poplar wood flooring made an ideal base upon which to keep house. For almost a month, they lived in the barn while the house was being renovated on its new foundation.

After the foundation was laid, the house was moved and secured into position. Two rooms were added on the east side. Will Pyle did all of the carpentry with the help of his brother, Clarence. Gradually, the house took shape. Maple trees were planted along the driveway and a woodshed built in the back. A "switcher," who used a willow twig to locate the water vein, located the site for the well. Despite a lot of digging and working, the water supply amounted to hardly more than a trickle. Will Pyle, years later, said the dowser must have been drinking.

Being the only baby in the midst of five adults brought Ernest Taylor Pyle much attention. Nothing was too good for little Ernest, as his mother respectfully referred to him. First it was a hobbyhorse, then fancy velvet clothes, little suits and knee britches, storybooks and fancy toys. Maria Pyle loved to sew and made all of Ernest's clothes in addition to many of those for the neighboring children. His hair was carrot orange, very full and fluffy. The neighbors would tell Taylor that little Ernest looked just like him, which brought the old gentleman even more joy in his later years.

During the long, hot summer, there was much canning and jelly making at the Pyle house. The neighbors shared their fruits and vegetables, so that no one would go hungry. Harry Bales had lots of gooseberries, Maiden Blush apples and currants; Doc Sturm had an abundance of cucumbers, which he grew on a lattice fence around the back porch; the Pyle family always had pole beans for canning; and George Bales had an abundance of grapes and pears.

The best strawberries came from John Taylor's patch. It was always an exciting day for Ernest to go with his parents to visit Uncle John and Aunt Lillie, as they lived about a 40-minute buggy ride southeast of the Mound at the intersection of two well-traveled gravel roads. When the strawberries were ripe, there was much traffic in that part of the country, as John and Lillie sold strawberries by the basketfuls.

When the blackberries were in season, this meant several berry-picking expeditions over to Uncle Oat's farm, which was the birthplace of Ernie's father. Behind the barn and back through the woods were vast patches of tangled blackberry vines. Using several milk buckets as the collecting station, Will, Maria, Ernest, the three youngest Saxton kids, Vivian, Sam, and, eventually, Lincoln, would each take a different path in search of fat and sweet blackberries. Covered with briar scratches and chigger bites, the procession would come back through the holler and across the foot log by the barn, collecting all of their buckets and pails near the well where they would admire their pickings for the day.

"Sam, you'd better see that Vivian and Lincoln take care of those chiggers," would remark Uncle Billie, who well knew that chiggers were a pesky part of picking blackberries. "Use some turpentine on them, Sam, that'll get 'em."

Since Oat Saxton had been a widower since the birth of Lincoln, his six children had taken care of the household chores. Maria Pyle watched over them and helped the girls with canning, sewing, and other feminine things. Lincoln, who was 4 years younger than Ernest, became a permanent ward of the Pyle household. As Maria often said, "That youngin' needs caring for." As another redheaded, freckled-faced kid, he fit neatly into the family pecking order. He was like a brother to Ernest, and an additional joy to his "Aunt Maria and Uncle Billy."

Once the Pyle family had returned to the Mound with their milk buckets brimming with freshly picked blackberries, Ernie's mother knew just how to handle the situation. "Will, you take Ernest out there to the cob house and get him washed off with some coal oil. He's got chigger bites all over his arms and legs." These were the usual instructions for post blackberry-picking trips. The treatment was an old one and seemed to help most of the time. The technique was rubbing a rag soaked with kerosene over the chigger areas. "I don't want him scratchin' and diggin' when we go to church tomorrow, Will."

Her face burned red from the hot sun, Maria immediately would start sorting out her cache of blackberries, as some would be canned for pies, some would be made into jam and some into blackberry jelly that went so good on hot biscuits on a cold morning. The big enameled teakettle was put on the stove, and next came bath time in the tub out back.

There were various kinds of jellies to be made. Maria Pyle was proud of her jelly cupboard. Little Ernest had a sweet tooth and his mother saw to it that the pantries of the Will Pyle and the George Bales households were well stocked. Ernest was very fond of strawberry jam, currant and raspberry jelly and preserves. Of course, there always was a good supply of blackberry, quince, grape, and apple jelly. It took a lot of sugar to put up these jellies and preserves, so on Saturday afternoons Will and Maria Pyle would drive the three miles to Dana where they would turn in their fresh cream and eggs to Jarvis Peer in exchange for produce at Lang's or Tom Clark's store. For this farm produce, they would get a 25-pound bag of sugar and the other staples needed for the kitchen.

Milking was a chore shared by Maria who loved to work with the livestock in the barn. She was a good milker and could fill a milk pail almost as fast as her husband, who was considered one of the best 'strippers' in the neighborhood. A 'squeezer' was the standard method of milking, whereby one squeezed the cow's teats with a full fist. But the 'stripper' separated the men from the boys because a milker using this technique used only the first finger and the thumb. In a fast motion, one would start at the cow's bag and strip down to the end of the teat. This was a fast way to milk, if one's forearm could take the strain. But Will Pyle was strong and wiry and he had been milking cows since he was knee high to a grasshopper.

Will hoped little Ernest would follow in his footsteps. He sure could use the help with the farm chores in a few years.

Chapter 5

Little Questions, Big Dreams

Ernest, as his parents always called him, liked the feel of the soil and the smell of the fresh earth. He and his mother regularly worked in the garden on the west side of the house. His father had made a hothouse box at the north end of the garden and, in early March, had planted tiny rows of tomatoes, cabbage, and bell pepper seeds. It was a pit, 3-feet by 4-feet across and 2-feet deep, covered tightly with a large-paneled window frame. The glass cover, tilted to the south, was banked high with dirt in order to keep out the cold March snow.

Will had plowed the garden in early spring with his walking plow as soon as the frost was out of the ground. Maria and Ernest transplanted fragile seedlings in neat rows across the garden. Before summer, the garden would produce an abundance of tomatoes, bunch beans, lima beans, radishes, lettuce, carrots, cabbage, onions, sweet potatoes, Irish potatoes, rhubarb, horseradish, and especially tender young garden peas, which Ernest liked cooked with new potatoes. What they didn't eat, they would store or can.

Ernest, now five years old, was a curious little boy and always asked many questions. He was particularly interested in trees.

"Doesn't it hurt the maple trees to bore holes in them and drain out the sap?" Ernie asked at the breakfast table on this early summer morning of 1906.

"No, because they provide us with a food in the form of maple syrup, which is part of God's plan," answered his mama.

"When Papa collects the maple water, how long do you cook it before it turns to molasses?"

"I cook it until it boils down thick. Sometimes it takes all day. When it starts to turn to syrup, I take it off the stove."

"It sure tastes good on your pancakes, Mama," said Ernest with a big smile, the empty fork in his right hand poised over the last bite of hot flapjacks.

"There are several sugar camps north of town. We bought some once from the Groves farm up on Jonathan Crick. They have a lot of trees. Our trees don't make that much syrup, but what they do make is awfully good," replied Maria, who always took the time to answer Ernest's questions.

The outdoors fascinated young Ernest. He was into everything. He would follow his father around like a shadow, especially when it came to hitching up the horses or plowing the garden or building the little hot bed for the early tomato plants. Almost before he could walk, his father let him drive the horses. At the age of three, his mother had showed him how to milk a cow. She taught him the "squeeze" technique, but now that he was five he had lost interest in the milking routine and dreaded having to clean the cow manure out of the stalls or feed the livestock.

Maria truly had only three real interests — her husband, little Ernest, and her farm work. She would rather drive a team of horses in the field than cook a dinner. Nothing else seemed to make much of a difference to her. Often she would daydream, imagining her young five-year-old in his late teens, leaving the farm forever. In her dreams, she was happy for him, proud that he had the courage to fly from the nest. He was at heart just like his daddy, she thought. Although Will had never lived anywhere except on a farm and although he would never admit it, he never liked life as farmer. He was a carpenter at heart, a wizard with tools. A quiet man, he never said a great deal. He never complained and seldom had to explain his behavior. Maria was pleased that Will didn't give Ernest advice, telling him to do this or do that. She took comfort in knowing that he didn't swear or drink or smoke, and that he was honest, in letter and in spirit. He was simply a good man without being annoying about his goodness.

Maria did little more than work hard and take care of her family, and yet she was happy. She had great faith that happiness can be found only within oneself. She would rather stay home and milk the cows than go to the state fair. She loved the farm and she loved Dana, Indiana (although she never thought of moving to town, as the other 'retired' farmers did). She was the best chicken raiser and cake baker in the neighborhood. And she made a promise she would do her best as a mother to teach little Ernest to be truly happy with himself, too . . . no matter where he may journey later in life.

Although Maria cared very little about world affairs, she was by far and away the broadest-minded and most liberal of the women in the county. She made a point never to tell Ernest that he couldn't do something. Her habit was simply to tell her young child what she thought was right and what she thought was wrong. She had confidence that Ernest would choose wisely and she guided him, letting him know the choice and the consequences would be up to him.

Maria Pyle was known for telling people just what she

thinks, and it's true that a good many of her neighbors felt the whip of her tongue. But whenever they were in trouble they always thawed out and came asking for help. And, of course, they would get it. Maria was the one neighbor always called on when somebody got sick, died, or needed help of any kind. She was the confidante of the young people around the county.

Growing up on a small Indiana farm, young Ernest Pyle quickly learned that there was a constant cycle to life; a time for planting and a time for harvesting, a time for life and a time for death. *The Farmer's Almanac* and human instinct were the guidelines Will and Maria depended on for scheduling the many diverse activities on the farm that involved man, nature, and animals.

Seasons came and went, the snow blew and the wind howled, and the rains pelted the fertile land. At five years old, Little Ernest had become more and more fearless because he was given greater and greater freedom to roam the countryside and explore the farm. Fearless, that is, with the exception of one thing — snakes!

Little Ernest had a horror of snakes. He wasn't afraid of being killed by a snake; it wasn't that kind of fear. It was a horrible, unnatural mania for getting away, for fleeing at the first sight of one of these creatures. It was a fear induced in equal measure by a 6-inch garden snake or a 6-foot black snake.

It was early Saturday morning, and Ernest had just finished his pancakes. "Mama, may I be excused? I want to go out to the field with Papa."

"Sure, Ernie, but be a help and not a hindrance," said Maria as Ernie sprinted out the kitchen door.

Will Pyle was plowing at the far end of the farm, a half-mile from the house. Little Ernest came along behind the plow, barefooted, in the fresh soft furrow. His dad had just started the field, and was plowing near a weedy fencerow. Red, wild roses were growing there.

"Papa, can I borrow your pocketknife," little Ernest asked. "I could cut some of those roses and take them back to the house for Mama."

Will smiled and reached in his overalls to retrieve his pocketknife. He gave it to his son without a word and went on plowing. Ernest sat down by the fence and started cutting off the roses. How happy Mama is going to be, he thought. Then, in a flash, it happened. A blue racer came looping through the tall grass directly towards Ernest. He screamed, threw the knife away, and ran as fast as he could away from the fence.

It was only moments later when he remembered his father's knife. Now, he realized, he was going to have to rustle up the courage and creep back over the plowed ground to find it. It was the bravest thing that the five-year-old had ever done, digging through the dirt and the tangle of weeds looking for that knife. He fully expected a snake to appear at any moment.

Will had heard little Ernest's scream and had stopped to watch his activity. He saw his son on his hands and knees searching for what he knew must be the knife. He walked over to Ernest. "What happened Ernest?" He could see the beginnings of a few tears, but there was no crying.

"A big snake scared me. I dropped the knife," he said, looking up for only a moment before returning to his search. "I'm sorry. I'm going to find it." A moment later, Ernie squealed, "Here it is!"

He picked up it up and proudly gave it to his dad. Then, with a bundle of fresh red roses in his hands, he set off for the house, the snake forgotten.

Little Ernest approached the garden from the west side. It was now grown up in high weeds. Looking at this new expanse of weeds to conquer, little Ernie once again became terrified. He stopped on the far side, and shouted for his mother, who was in the kitchen, cleaning up. She stepped outside and saw him across the garden.

"Mama, please come and get me," he pleaded.

"Ernest, you get yourself moving and come on through those weeds right now!"

All little Ernest could think was that he couldn't do it even if it was going to kill him not to.

"If you don't stop crying, and come on through, I'm going to have to whip you," his mother shouted over the top of the weeds. Of course, this made him cry even harder. He dropped the bundle of roses on the ground. He couldn't stop crying and his legs wouldn't move.

His mother marched through the weeds and picked him up. She whipped him. It was one of the two times she would ever lay a hand in anger on him.

That evening, when Will came in from the fields, Maria told him about their crazy boy who wouldn't walk through the weeds. "I don't know what was wrong with the boy. I am so sorry, but I had to be whip him, Will," she said.

And then Will told her about the knife. And the snake. And the roses. When she heard the part about the roses, she was silenced. She said very little for the rest of the day, and she cried for a long time that night when she went to bed.

The next day, Sunday, all was forgotten and everyone got up excited about dinner. Summer was fried chicken time, and this Sunday was going to be a great event for the neighbors. Dinner at the Pyle home during summer didn't change much over the years; you always had a fairly good idea of what the menu would be. "Dinner" was the main meal at noontime, and "supper" came after all of the stock and chickens were fed and locked up for the night. A typical Sunday dinner in the summer, which was special, would be fried chicken and gravy, mashed potatoes, maybe fresh garden peas if they turned out that season, carrots from the garden, or, one of Ernie's favorites, wilted lettuce. (In the winter it was baked hen with egg noodles.)

To prepare the wilted lettuce, Ernie's mother would clean a big pile of lettuce fresh from the north end of the garden and put it in a heavy serving dish. Over this she would pour a very hot mixture of real apple vinegar and water, mixed with sugar and salt. Then she would put a dinner plate over the bowl to let it "wilt." At the very last moment, she would add some little green onions, some red and white radishes, and maybe a few scraps of already cooked bacon.

Cooking chicken was one of Ernie's mother's specialties. Today, Ernie sat on the kitchen window ledge where he would have an excellent vantage point for observing the chef in action. She used a large black skillet with matching lid. To begin with she would go out on the back porch where it was cool and take off the lid of a five-gallon can of white lard. A big fistful of white lard would be melted in the skillet, and when it started popping a little, she would drop in the floured pieces of chicken until the skillet was brimming full. After she had browned each piece, artfully turning them in sequence, she would remove the skillet to the back of the stove where it wasn't so hot then let the chicken simmer along. The liver was always put in last, as it usually popped and splattered hot grease.

Next she would pour most of the hot grease left in the skillet into a large container of used lard. Now came the chicken gravy. In her cupboard in the corner, she kept a tin box with flour in it. She would reach her big hand into the box and get a handful of flour, which she would sift into the skillet. Some milk, salt and pepper were added, and the gravy was on the way.

"Here, you watch the gravy, and don't let it get too thick," she instructed Ernie. "Keep stirring it and add some milk if you have to." Ernie thought he probably had stirred more skillets of chicken gravy than any kid in Indiana. But that was part of living on the farm.

Raising chickens was also a necessary part of living on the farm. This was the housewife's primary source of income. The Pyle family became so sophisticated that they borrowed an incubator set-up in the corner of their dining room, where the chickens were hatched without the natural use of the hen. Will had constructed a nice brooder house for the newly hatched chicks, which had a kerosene heater in it. The Pyle family went in big for the Rhode Island Reds. So Maria Pyle, a true entrepreneur, had a good corner on the local chicken market.

Everyone had a part in preparing the meal. There always was a fresh bucket of water needed from the well, or chairs to be set up around the table, or the water glasses to be checked or even the salt and pepper shakers to be filled.

Most of the men at family gatherings drank iced tea during the summer. It was prepared with just a handful of loose tea boiled in a pan. The ice had to be chipped off the block of ice in the old icebox, which stood out on the back porch. A fifty-pound block of ice would last for several days in the oak cooler.

After the meal, the men gathered on the porch, Ernie's mother brought out iced tea while little Ernest chipped away at the block for extra ice. She told everyone the story of how Ernest was so sweet to bring her roses but that she didn't understand how scared he was and why he wouldn't cross the old garden. Toward the end of the story, she managed to get the hem of her apron up around her eyes, just in case she should need it, which she did.

Ernie and his mother cleaned up the porch and got everything back into order. After a moment or two they both sat down and looked out on the beautiful countryside. For five or ten minutes they sat in contented silence, the whipping and the snake completely forgotten. "Mama," asked the inquisitive young Ernest, "what makes the maple sap come up the trees?"

Maria adjusted her apron and tugged on her sunbonnet. She spoke gently to her son. "If the sap stayed above ground all winter, you know it would freeze during those cold spells. God worked out a plan for every plant and animal to survive. The sap of the maple is the spirit of the tree, and to protect that spark of life, God has the sap stored deep underground where it is safe during the cold winter months. Then when the days start getting warm in the springtime and the sun starts moving back north, something tells the sap to come up out of the ground and make the trees grow new leaves."

"What makes seeds grow?"

"God puts a spark of life in each seed so, at the right time, the right temperature, and the right soil, it sprouts and reproduces".

"The dirt makes them grow?"

"Yes, and the rain. A tiny seed can stay stored for many, many years, yet the spark of life in it will still be alive. You've seen your father sort out the seed corn there on the back porch and from every ear, he takes out a kernel and bites off the tip end. He is just checking to see that the heart of the kernel is alive. If it's yellow, it's all right, if it is real dark, then he throws out that ear of corn."

"How deep does this dirt go?"

"It goes all the way through the earth, I guess."

"What's on the other side of the earth?"

"More dirt and more people, Ernest."

"Mama, if Thad and I dig a hole out here in the garden and it went clear through the earth, where would it come out?"

"I guess you'd come out in China someplace."

"Where's China?"

"China is in the Orient."

Little Ernest thought about that for a moment. "Are they like us?"

"Yes, but they are different, too; they have slanted eyes and their skin is yellow."

"Gosh, I hope someday I get to see them!"

"Maybe you will someday, Ernest, but it is a long voyage to the Orient, and there isn't anyone around Dana that I know of who has been there. After you finish high school, maybe you can get a job and save your money and go to the Orient."

"Mama, it would take an awful lot of money, wouldn't it?"

"Yes, Ernest, an awful lot," said Maria as she stood up and walked over to the porch steps. "Here, go fetch me a bucket of water so we can go water the tomato plants."

Ernie, bucket in hand, may have been on his way to the well, but in his imagination he was on a great journey, on his way to discover the wondrous people and the mysterious expanse called China.

Chapter 6

The Potter Boys

It was 1906. Fall was in the air. The apple orchard out back had just started producing and, now, little Ernest was all set for first grade. Starting school was a major event at the Pyle household. At the age of six, all able-bodied children in Vermillion County were required to attend school. The Bono School, known as the Helt Township High School (even though it had all 12 grades), was just down the road a ways and had opened in 1904. Dana still had a commissioned school with all 12 grades. Since the Pyle family lived in the county, they could send Ernie to either school.

Iva Jordan, the first-grade teacher, lived only a mile up the road on the way to town. After talking with neighbors, Maria Pyle decided that little Ernest should go to the Dana school, at least for his first year. Maria made arrangements with Harry and Tott Bales, who lived at the Caleb Bales place, for Ernest to ride with Mariam Bales and Carl Crane, who were also entering the first grade. Carl was a nephew of Harry Bales, and when his mother died, he had moved in with the Bales family. For almost the entire first-grade, Ernie, Mariam, and Carl rode back and forth together in a one-horse buggy or sometimes on Mariam's pony.

For Ernest to get to the Dana school, he had to join up with his group by riding his pony over to the Bales' place. He always arrived a little early because he had to put the pony in the barn for the day. He would put it in the north stall, which Harry had saved just for him.

It was often said that Mariam Bales was Ernest's puppy love, and Ernie took the teasing in stride. One morning, as he was waiting for his group, Ernie took out his pocketknife and carved "E.P. + M.B." into the side of the horse stall. "I hope these initials stay here forever," Ernie thought to himself. He really did like Mariam. He didn't care if everyone knew it. "It's the truth," Ernie thought, "and Mama and Papa always say to tell the truth."

Being a first grader was quite a challenge for Ernest; he was an only child and it was his first time away from his mother. Although it was only three miles to the Dana schoolhouse, it seemed like ten to the young boy. Sometimes his riding group would stop in town after school to look around and even occasionally pick up some goods from the hardware store for the Bales or the Pyle family. As time wore on, Ernie, Carl, and Mariam each got more familiar with the surroundings and the townsfolk. Little Ernest, however, began to realize he might not ever feel completely at ease with the big city life.

"Dana is a pretty town," he told his mother one afternoon at the end of the school year. The summer was just beginning and they were sitting on the porch. "I mean the streets are pretty when you look down them, especially now that it's summer." Nearly every street in Dana was a cool, dark tunnel formed by the great maple trees on either side. "But, Mama, is there something wrong with being a farm boy? The town kids make fun of me and make me feel bad."

Maria Pyle looked at her only child with great concern.

"Ernest, people who have been around say Dana is a medium good town. I really don't know whether it is or not," said his mother. "I haven't traveled too much."

"Every time I walk down the street, I think the bigger boys are laughing at me. I don't like that feeling at all."

She was relieved that it was nothing more than teasing. "Ernie, time heals all wounds. Just put it behind you, and move on." She pulled him close and hugged him hard.

Ernie's second-grade year was soon upon him. It was much more convenient for the neighborhood children to attend the Bono School, so most of the parents, including Maria and Will Pyle, decided that from that time forward their children would attend the Bono school. Men in the community would take turns driving the horse-drawn school hacks to get the children to school.

The community around the Mound was awash with kids, and new families and faces were moving in all the time. The Taylor household seemed ever more crowded, even though Ernie was still the only child among the five adults: his parents, Will and Maria, his grandfather, Lambert Taylor, his uncle John, and his aunt Mary.

Ernie's uncle John was a tall, handsome man who could quote the Bible even better than his father, Lambert. Uncle John attended church regularly and taught the young men's Sunday school class. Taylor was concerned that neither John, his only son, nor Mary, his eldest daughter, had found suitable mates. But, thankfully, it was through his association with the church, that John met a fair young maiden by the name of Lilly Pearman, a bright and pretty girl, several years his younger. This acquaintance soon ended up in a fine marriage, freeing up much-needed room at the Mound. And it wouldn't be long before Mary would be joining the ranks of the married, too.

There was much joy over John Taylor's wedding. John and Lilly moved to a nearby farm, below Oll Staats corner, and started a humble but proud household. Samuel Edwin Taylor arrived on a cold blustery day, the 26th of November 1908, with the help of Doc Keys and Maria Pyle as mid-wife. Now Lambert had two grandsons, and the latter carried the Taylor name. Had Lambert lived long enough, he would have seen his Samuel grow up to be a prominent educator, marrying the neighbor girl, Ilo Elizabeth, and producing four sons bearing the Taylor name. But Lambert died in 1911 and was buried in Helt Cemetery. The Taylors were good people. They worked hard, supported each other, and kept the Sabbath holy. Lambert Taylor left a proud legacy.

People moved a lot in those days, as the country was beginning to open up and there was lots of work on the farms. The railroad coming through Dana added several new businesses to the community. Frank Kuhns and his wife moved into the old Houchin place, which his parents, Henry and Mary Kuhns, had bought from Bruce Houchin. It had a small log barn near the house, similar to the barn at the Taylor farm, the Mound, next door. Frank and Lelia Kuhns were about the same age as Will and Maria Pyle, so they became not only close neighbors, but also fast friends.

Lelia Kuhns bore ten children while living there: Everett, Leslie, Frank, Mary Alice, Fern, Clara Bell, Edna, Paul, Bob, and Nellie. Because of the growing traffic between the two neighbors, Will Pyle decided to build a stile over the fence, just east of his barn, and Frank started plans for building a new two-story house for his expanding family in 1911, the same year that Lambert Taylor died.

As a result of such a large extended family of friends and neighbors, Ernie's mother soon became the community mid-wife. Whether it was a new calf, lamb, or baby, she was there for the delivery. She assisted with the birth of every one of the Kuhns kids, with the exception of Paul.

Maria loved her new role in the community, and so did little Ernest! Newborns became such a fascination to the young Ernest Pyle that he would go visiting a family the very next day after a child was born to get a peek at the new baby his mother had helped to bring into the world. In her own patient and gentle manner, Ernie's mother taught him great respect for new life . . . and for newcomers.

The Potters were the poorest of all the boys in the neighborhood. "The Potter boys talk funny, Mama," Ernie said one day. The Potter family had just arrived from the Kentucky hills, and they seldom smiled. "Me and Thad want to make friends, but they're always busy finding work and don't seem too interested."

The Potters had just moved into the old Keys place, which had been purchased by Dr. John Sturm, the Purdue veterinarian, who owned land south of the Pyle farm. Dan Potter and his wife had three boys: George, Oll, and Charlie. Although they started out poor and had a very difficult time making ends meet, the Potter family would quickly become a great asset to the community.

"Ernest, give them a chance," said his mama. "They're just like anybody else. You'll see. They'll come around once they figure out what's what and who's who around these parts."

George Potter was the oldest boy in the Potter clan, and even at an early age he had a keen business mind. He quickly landed a job helping George Bales around his farm. He did odd jobs for him for over a year and saved every penny he made. He was a hard worker. When George Bales asked him one day how it was that a boy of his age could work so hard, the young Potter said with a grin on his face he wanted to see Chicago someday. Now that the Bales and the Potters had become such close friends, little Ernest, who visited his Aunt Mary Bales regularly, developed a fondness for the Potter boys, too. It wasn't long before they fit right in with the neighborhood gang and were included in all of the local goings-on.

The school hack would pick up Ernest and the Kuhns kids on the way to Bono; then it would turn south at the Mound and pick up the Potter boys just a quarter of a mile south of the old Keys place. In wasn't long before George Potter taught Ernest, now at the tender age of nine, how to chew tobacco. George showed Ernest how to hang off the back step of the horse-drawn hack and spit tobacco juice at the rocks as they passed them by.

Down in the pasture in front of the Kuhns house was the old Mound schoolhouse. It had been closed and boarded up since the turn of the century after serving the community for 31 years. Mr. Kuhns kept it boarded up and used it to store grain. It was one of the oldest school buildings in that part of Indiana and was even in good condition in 1938 when it was torn down. It served as base of operations for the boys.

The east side of the Mound was a great place to play, and the kids came from far and wide to join in the fun. On most any Sunday afternoon, after dinner, one could find little Ernie Pyle with his bigger friends, Ed Goforth, Paul Sturm, Carl Crane, Thad Hooker, Bill Bales, Homer Ingram, Sam Saxton, Lincoln Saxton, and the Kuhns kids. And now the Potter boys.

Baseball was perhaps the most favorite "organized" sport,

of course, but rolling an old buggy chassis down the hill could be just as much fun. And they often organized Indian hunting parties and charged up the Mound through the locust trees. Rumor had it, after all, that the Mound was an ancient Indian burial ground.

Another place to visit was the Bales' cemetery. They marched through the woods behind the barn at the Campbell farm, across Harry Bales' orchard, and over to the cemetery where they counted the Civil War headstones and read the epitaphs. Then they would go over to Mr. Webster's pasture and stage mock battles between the North and the South. Little Ernie was happy to be the private and never the general.

These boyhood days were great years for Ernie. In his third year of school, Ernest made a lifelong friend in Thad Hooker, who also had red hair and was about as skinny as Ernest.

Thad lived a mile and a half west of the Mound. They became inseparable pals. He and Ernest played wild games, imagined they were Knights of the Round Table, and raced their ponies up and down the dusty roads.

Ernest had a small bay mare. The other horses at the Pyle farm were heavy workhorses and were not the running kind. But Ernest's mare was named "Betsy" and she was smaller-boned than the heavier horses. When he and Thad went on one of their many riding escapades, his mother always was concerned that something might happen to the boys, but they were both good riders and could saddle their own horses.

When Ernest turned ten, he got a new saddle from Montgomery Ward in Chicago. It was a birthday present from his father. His mother gave him a heavy piece of wool to use as a saddle blanket. Ernie had to saddle up his own steed and cinch the saddle tight so it wouldn't roll. He learned basic horsemanship but sometimes overextended his little mare when he was racing her down the roadways near the Mound. One time he came back to the house with a lathered and sweating horse; his mother jerked him out of the saddle. "Ernie, I don't believe you appreciate Betsy," she scolded. "Horses are very powerful creatures, and you're going to have to learn to respect their power." She instructed him to wash Betsy down and to groom her real good with the curry brush.

Perhaps the most favorite of all the pastimes the boys enjoyed was when they would take a trek down to Mr. Webster's pasture, where they would play in the creek and climb the big oak trees along the ditch. During the hot summer months, they would fish and swim in Mr. Webster's pasture where the creek dribbled through the woodlands. It was a great way of life for a farm boy.

One day in early July, after breakfast, little Ernest and George got together and decided to go fishing. They walked, barefooted, of course, down the road half a mile or so to the creek in Mr. Webster's pasture. Ernie and George and the rest of their buddies had fished in this creek hundreds of times. It was not that big. You could jump across it almost any place. It was often muddy, though, and grass had now grown up all along the banks.

The boys followed the creek a ways as it snaked across the bluegrass pasture in-between occasional oak trees. A loose gathering of shorthorn cows, munching contentedly, turned to stare at them. "I sure am glad Mr. Webster sold that big Guernsey bull," said George. Bob Webster had a very productive farm, and his prize bull was one of the biggest in the county. And, as far as the boys were concerned, it was the meanest. One time, several of the boys were playing along the creek on the other side of Webster's pasture. The big bull, wild-eyed and snorting, rammed into the split-rail fence so hard it shattered one of the sturdy rails. Of course, the boys didn't stick around long enough to see if the bull managed to get out!

"Ernie," said the much bigger George Potter, "I believe there are fish right there." He was pointing at a hole that must have been five feet across, and maybe two feet deep. George had gotten up early that morning and had dug worms for the occasion. He had put them in a Prince Albert tobacco can, which he was just now pulling out of the hip pocket of his overalls.

"Ernie, I been thinking," he said.

George was a big guy who didn't like to say a whole lot. He paused between sentences and never seemed concerned about making his point quickly. George thought long and hard about things, and when he talked, people really listened. Next to Thad, George was the one friend Ernie looked up to and whose opinion he valued the most.

Ernie, on the other hand, was always the little joker. "George, you know it makes me uncomfortable when you start to thinking." He couldn't pass up an opportunity to tease his friend about his silent demeanor.

George remained expressionless. "Ernie, I got us exactly 26 worms in this Prince Albert can." He had taken the circular tin cap off the top of the container and was holding out the can of worms to show Ernie.

"The last time you and I fished in this creek, George, you didn't even know how to bait a hook," Ernie joked again. Trying to get George to smile was always a great game for Ernie.

"Ernie, we're gonna have ourselves a fishing contest," said George without looking up. "We each get thirteen worms and between the both of us we have to catch a dozen fish." George started counting out the worms. "That's it, 26 worms, a dozen fish. If we can't do that, we ain't got the right to call ourselves fishermen."

George picked up the stick he had selected from a willow tree growing along the bank near the fishing whole, and started towards the creek where Ernie was already shoving the first worm on his hook. "Ernie, you gonna feel sorry for that worm or are you gonna try and catch some fish?" George Potter teased Ernie, watching him curiously.

Although it may have looked as if Ernie couldn't bear to hurt the worm, he finally succeeded in getting it on his hook, made from one of Aunt Mary's straight pins, which he had bent on his papa's anvil back at the barn. He spit on the bait and threw his line in the creek.

"How much you wanna bet I catch the first fish?" Ernie asked.

"A nickel," George said, rising to the challenge.

In one swift action, George baited his hook and threw his line in right next to Ernie's. George's cork never even stopped at the surface. It just went right on down. George gave the pole a slight jerk, and out came the first fish of the day, a little sunfish about as long as your finger. It hadn't been three seconds. "Forget about the nickel, Ernie; let's just catch fish." George threw the fish back in; it was too little to keep, but it counted towards the contest.

For the next hour or so, Ernie and George sat there on the bank, with George pulling in keepers, one by one. He caught seven straight after the first one, for a total of eight fish. On his next two tries, he lost his bait both times. "I think it's about time we took a break," he said.

Ernie had now lost his bait nine times without catching a fish. "You go ahead," he said to George, "I feel lucky." Ernie tossed in his line, and after only a few seconds, the bobber went under. Ernie tugged and set the hook. "Finally," Ernie yelled, but just as he reached for the fish, it threw the hook and flopped back into the water. "I lost him!" shouted Ernie to the treetops. George thought about telling him he was trying too hard, but then decided Ernie wasn't really asking a question.

Ernie's mother had put a couple of apples into the burlap bag the boys carried with them. She also cut them a hunk of cheese and had put it in a bread wrapper. The boys settled down on a shady, grassy spot close to the fishing hole. It lay underneath an old oak and they were happily surprised when a slight breeze stirred up from the west. It was the perfect lazy summer day.

George was about to say something to Ernie when all of a sudden he leaped up and ran to the bank. He fumbled for the stringer of fish they had caught and once he got a hold of it, he yanked it out of the water and slung it on the ground beside him. "Did you see the size of that snappin' turtle?" he asked Ernie. Snapping turtles have powerful jaws and can bite a kids finger off as easily as a monkey biting a banana. Moments before, a snapping turtle had just quietly slipped off the far bank into the water. "That turtle was after our stringer for sure. We were gonna go home with a bunch of fish heads!" said George.

They sat there eating their apples and cheese. After they each had a few bites, George finally said, "Ernie, someone shot my dog yesterday."

Ernie never thought he would see one of his friends cry without at least being injured in some way. Especially big, tough George Potter. But Ernie could see tears welling up in both eyes. George quickly looked away.

Most boys in the county, including Ernie, had a dog they cared for, a dog that roamed the countryside at one time or another. "What happened, George," Ernie asked, knowing that most farmers knew whose dog was whose and, even if not, could usually tell the difference between a dog that was cared for and a dog that was part of a pack. Scrawny strays traveled in packs and for the most part they stayed close to town, scavenging trash. Farmers had the right to shoot dogs that threatened their livestock. They weren't going to put up with a pack of dogs killing their sheep.

"Well, we were havin' Sunday dinner and were just about finished. Mama was clearin' the table and we was all waitin' for pie." George kept looking at the ground, drawing circles in the dirt. He didn't say anything more for about a minute or two. Ernie knew George well enough to wait. "Next thing I know, we all hear a shotgun blast in the distance," said George. "Daddy said it sounded like one of our neighbors just killed a dog." George looked straight at Ernie. "It wasn't till later that day I learnt it was my dog and that it was old man Elder who probably done it. He knew it was my dog, Ernie, but shot it anyway," George said, shaking his head as if he still couldn't believe it. "He knew it weren't no stray."

Ernie didn't know what to say. They both just sat there in silence for a few minutes.

"I'm sorry, George, . . ." Ernie started to say more, but,

George quickly piped up, "All right, I got four more worms and you got three. We've caught eight fish so far, so, let's see, we got to catch four more fish with seven worms."

George looked at Ernie and smiled. "You ready to become a fisherman?"

In the next ten minutes, George caught three fish and Ernie lost two worms. They each had one worm remaining and only needed one fish to reach their challenge. George and Ernie both got real serious. They looked at each other and for the first time they felt the pressure of having to succeed. George said, "Ernie, this is our last chance. We can't go home without the twelfth fish." Ernie just nodded. They both put their lines in the water.

After several minutes, George felt a tug. He let the fish tug on it one more time and then, on the third strike, he whipped the willow stick back over his right shoulder just a little too hard. The fish fell of the hook just as it was breaking the surface. The hook was without a worm, and it was now up to Ernie, who hadn't caught a fish the entire day.

Ernie had never felt such pressure. He knew he couldn't let his friend down. He concentrated on the fishing line, trying to imagine a fish approaching the bait. After a few minutes, he checked his line to make sure it was still on the hook. It was. He put it back in the water and waited.

He was amazed when his bobber went under . . . and stayed under! He barely moved his wrist, hoping against hope to set the hook. Ernie saw that, yes, he had a fish! Somehow he got it out of the water and onto the bank. George slapped him on the back. Both were truly amazed to see the largest sunfish of the day. "Ernie," said George, "my daddy says we all get our chances in life and you gotta take 'em when you get 'em. Well, you just lived up to one of yours."

Ernie took that fish home and cleaned it. Even though it was not much bigger than his hand, Ernie told his mama that it was all he wanted for supper. And later that night, before he went to bed, he said a prayer for a good fishing buddy and his dog and the man who shot it.

The Potter boys toiled and saved their money, and all grew up knowing how to work. The whole county admired them for the way they raised themselves by the bootstraps.

Dan Potter, the father, taught them well. He would work all day for 50 cents doing the hardest kind of manual labor. Some of the wealthier farmers took advantage of him and worked him until he would almost drop. But with three boys and a wife to feed, he had no choice.

Most of the large homes along Main Street were heated with large coal burning furnaces in the basement, thus requiring a full bin of good coal to make it through the long winter. A wealthy cattle and hog farmer with a very large house on Main Street, once asked the young newcomer, Oll Potter, if he could get him a load of coal from St. Bernice, a distance of some eleven miles. Oll would be paid $2 for the trouble.

Oll borrowed Claude Lockridge's Model T truck for this $2 opportunity. He filled up the truck bed with coal and parked it just outside the north basement window of the big house. All afternoon he shoveled the coal, scoop by scoop, out of the truck, through the basement window and into the coal bin. It was backbreaking work. But that $2 was a fortune to Oll. He was the middle of the Potter boys, a six-foot-four bony giant of a kid, who was used to hard physical work. As the cold northwestern wind whipped through the trees and darkness started to settle over the town like a black overcoat, Oll knocked on the big glass-paneled door to collect his money.

At first, he thought that maybe he wasn't knocking loud enough, so he tried a second and a third time. Finally, the man cracked his front door. "We're having supper now, Oll. Can you come back tomorrow?" he asked.

"I reckon so," Oll replied.

"I'll talk to you then," came a curt reply from behind the door.

The next day, when Oll went back to collect his $2, the stuffy little man said he would like for him to shovel out that load of coal and take it back. "I'm afraid I've found a better buy down near Blanford."

Oll didn't say a word, but borrowed the truck again, shoveled out the entire load of coal, back up and out of the basement window and finally into the truck.

He never collected on his $2.00!

But, the Potters had good neighbors and everyone tried to help them along. They would take on any job and they were happy and optimistic in the process. George would later become the fiscal manager of the Potter brother's expanding business, especially their land, gravel, and elevator operations. Oll, the big gentle giant, later became the sheriff of Vermillion County. Charlie supervised the Potter farms and livestock programs, and was everybody's friend. It was said that Charlie Potter himself paid for the funerals of several of the homeless and aged old men in Dana. Charlie knew poverty and he was happy to share a square meal with a bottle of beer with the poor and out-of-luck. He was their friend, too, and always would be.

Chapter 7

Aunt Mary Bales

Gradually, the Taylor farm at the Mound became more comfortable with each passing year. The dining room and kitchen were much-needed additions to the original house. Will Pyle was an excellent cabinetmaker and general carpenter, so he added cupboards, shelves, and even a new outside entrance doorway in the dining room. Will started building on the south porch, which would run almost the full length of the house. More and more acreage had been cleared for farming, and since all of the farms in the community needed repairs and new buildings, Will Pyle was able to get a lot of work helping out. Times were good for the Pyle and Taylor families.

Lambert Taylor was a proud man and he wanted only the best for his family. He figured his son-in-law could work for his room and board. With the continuous flow of money received for the gravel he sold, there was a constant building and improvement program underway at the Taylor farm. Taylor bought wagonloads of good lumber from Pawley's lumberyard in Dana. Will Pyle not only worked in the fields, but, also, after the barnyard chores were completed, he picked up his tools and went to work as a carpenter. Maria worked along side her new husband, as she thoroughly enjoyed the out-of-doors work.

Each fall, Ernest's mama and his Aunt Mary would stuff large bell peppers with a mixture of chopped cabbage, pimentos, salt, pepper and sugar, dill seed and onions. These would be stacked carefully in layers, after the tops had been secured on each with a toothpick, in a five-gallon crock jar. Ernest's mother would heat up a mixture of fresh cider vinegar and water on top of the stove until it was ready to boil. She would then fill up the tall jar to the brim with the hot mixture. After the round wooden lid was put in place, the big jar was put in a cool place and left to season during the long winter months.

Ernest liked to run the long yellow ears of corn through the corn sheller and see the white cobs fly out the far end as he spun the big wheel. The cobs were dried and then saved for starting the morning fire in the kitchen stove. He was a cob fancier and even made his own corncob pipe. He and the neighbor boys had numerous corncob fights around the barn. For heavier missiles, he and Thad Hooker would soak theirs in a bucket of water. Cob fights were great fun. Occasionally, a tomcat at the barn would get into the line of fire and go scurrying up into the haymow for refuge.

After the first frost, Will and Maria would store food supplies for the bleak and disagreeable winter season. Indiana winters could be bitterly cold and lonesome. The cabbage was stored underground at the north end of the garden in a hole lined with straw. Will and Ernest would dig a hole about three feet deep and four feet across, then line the hole with straw. Into this cavity was thrown several dozen heads of hard, crisp cabbage from the late planting. Another layer of straw, then an old blanket was laid on top. Finally, all of the excavated dirt was piled on top. The cabbage would now keep until springtime.

Under the watchful eye of Maria, the sixteen apple trees planted in the chicken yard started bearing. Maria used green apples for pies and cobblers, red ones for jelly. To protect the apples from the winter cold, two bushels were kept in the pantry for eating, while the rest were buried along side the cabbage. The apples were nestled inside a heavy tarpaulin filled with straw. Several bushels could be saved this way as they remained underground. There was a small access hole on the south side of the cache of apples for retrieval. It was Ernest's chore to dig out the apples for the household needs, invariably during the coldest part of the winter. These cold Winesaps and Jonathans had a strong and delicious apple fragrance to them when brought indoors.

As all farm boys know early in life, the call of the sod gets to one sooner or later. Farming back in the early 1900s was done almost completely by horses. It was the mark of manhood when the boys in the family started working in the fields. Ernie was no exception.

At the age of nine, he was riding an Oliver sulky plow behind three workhorses. While plowing near some of the old stumps on the west side of the house, a big, fat groundhog, which had been sleeping on top of one of the stumps, jumped off and scurried for his den when the horses approached. That was all it took to scare the team. Ernie suddenly found himself thrown off the back of the plow, the horses rearing and entangled in their harness. They almost ran away with him! His mother, always afraid that something would happen to him, heard the commotion and rushed outside in the fear that he had had a terrible accident with the farm equipment. She was relieved to find Ernie settling the horses, but, after this episode, little Ernest's days as a young and budding farmhand were numbered.

There were lots of horses in the community, and occasionally, one would hear of a runaway team that tore up the harness and the wagon and even injured the driver. A spooky horse was something to stay away from, as Ernie learned early in life.

Will then made plans for another addition to the back porch so Maria could have a place to store the milk and cream carried in milk buckets from the barn each morning. There was constant building to do; Will's carpentry was just what was needed to make the home more comfortable. Even though Ernie's Uncle John had married and had moved with his wife, Lilly, into his own home, there still wasn't much space for their crowded family of three generations. But events would soon lead to Ernie's Aunt Mary moving out for good.

Births, marriages and funerals made up for most of the community entertainment. Each was a ceremony, and the neighbors would turn out in full force. It was a time for laughing and crying, a time for singing and story telling, and a time to visit the neighbors you hadn't had a chance to see in a few months.

⊷══◉◒⊷

Just a mile and a half west of the Mound was the George Bales farm. William Franklin Bales, born in 1892, "Willie" for short, was one of Ernie's mentors. Willie was named after his grandfather William Bales, whose father was George Bales. Willie's grandfather, George Bales, had bought the farm just before the Civil War.

By the time he was 10, he was in the fourth grade. He attended the Old Mound School until it closed. He then finished at Helt Township High School in Bono, just two miles south. When he was in the third grade, he and Homer Ingram caught a young flying squirrel in the woods and took it to school in a box hidden inside Willie's shirt. Once the box was opened, the squirrel flew around the room, bouncing off the walls, and trying to escape. It broke up the one-room class and the teacher sent Willie home.

Willie rode his horse by the Taylor place at the Mound every day he went to school. He liked to stop and visit with his uncle, Dr. John Sturm, who became one of his best friends in the years to come. Dr. Sturm's beautiful wife was Willie's father's sister. He was quite sure of getting a cookie or two if he stopped by.

At the age of 12, in 1904, he was a rather scared looking lad with ruddy face and home-cropped hair. He was growing tall and almost reached his father's shoulder. The neighbors who kept coming by in their buggies, often remarked how sad and bashful the little boy was. He had reason to be sad. His mother was dying.

His father had told him she was dying. He would stand by his mother's bedside when he came in from school and tell her about his lessons. He loved to hear the stories she told, but she became more ill each day. Finally, she could not tell him stories as she was so wracked with pain.

One day a very large, black piano arrived and was placed in the west parlor where it sat forever. That was a day he would never forget, for his mother was brought into the parlor where she tried to play the new piano, but she was just too weak and frail. His mother was not an ordinary woman - she had been a tall, beautiful lady, but she was just too weak to play the music they wanted to hear. She had been poorly for months, and now she was bedridden. Willie didn't know just what that meant, but he knew she was dying and there was nothing a 12-year-old boy could do about it. .

In 1905, the boy's mother left this old world and the son thought he would never love anyone again. The day of the funeral came. Willie hid at the far end of the apple orchard while the neighbors came and went continuously. In those days, when a person passed on, the neighbors came in and made the burial clothes. They dressed Virginia Vaness Bales all in white and the undertaker came and lifted her frail body into the casket. And the people came and went.

A black hearse drawn by two horses had stopped at the front gate, and crowds of people in their buggies arrived. Willie remained in the bushes, and clearly heard his father calling his name. He must get away. He wasn't going to watch his mother put into the ground! He ran across the fields, the roadway and across the creek until he reached the woods. He hid there the entire day until someone found him toward evening, his face wet with tears and his tousled head buried against a tree.

Willie would sit on the well platform for hours and watch the big windmill high above him slowly turn round and round as it pumped water for the horses and cows behind the barn. He spent a lot of time talking to his sorrel trotting mare, named Helen after his favorite schoolteacher. He didn't want to play with the other boys in the neighborhood. They had mothers and fathers.

His father, George Bales, was a lost and saddened man without his wife, for whom he had bought that big square piano as a last show of tender affection. Thankfully, he had friends and family to see him through. His brother, Frank, lived just east at the next farm, and just beyond that came Harry Bales farm and the woods. Beyond the woods going east was the small 7-acre Campbell farm worked by Clarence Campbell ever since his return from the Civil War. His frail wife, Sarah, bore him five children - Clarence, Rex, Sadie, Lucy and Helen.

But George Bales carried his great sorrow alone, day after day, for many months. He knew he could not care adequately for his son Willie, now 13, but someone must do it. George Bales had a strong body and a strong voice. He cooked three meals, and when the good and kind neighbors did not bring in a pie or cake, or perhaps a fried chicken, he would fry meat and potatoes served with black coffee. He tried to keep the house clean, too, but it was all just too much for a man to do. He would always return to the field and work even harder to keep from thinking of the woman he had loved so much.

During the following summers, Willie worked with his father on the farm. Willie liked the animals, particularly the horses. One day there was great news in the neighborhood. He learned that his father was going to marry a maiden lady about his father's age. She was going to move in with them on the farm. She would be his second mother. She asked that he call her "Mary" and she called him "Bill." She would fix ice cream and fried chicken for him and she washed and ironed his clothes. She was jolly, a good cook, very neat and very active. He grew to love his new mother, Mary, and it was quickly observed by one and all how he was now such a happy young man.

Aunt Mary was Ernie's best friend and almost as close to him as his own mother. After all, she had lived at the Mound with Maria and Will, her father Lambert Taylor, and with little Ernest until 1908. She had been Ernie's constant companion and help-mate since his birth.

Ernie's Aunt Mary, as everyone called Mary Elizabeth Taylor, was one of a kind. She was a rescuer. Not only had she doted on Ernie as if he were her own son for over eight years, she sought out and would care for anyone and everyone in need or in pain. So, it was not surprising when she set her sights on the widowed George Bales and his teenage son, William.

It was destined that Aunt Mary and George Bales get married, both in their 40s, and with a lonesome 16 year old boy in the house. It happened on September 23, 1908, at the Bono Methodist Church, where the Reverend J. L. Greenway tied the knot.

Aunt Mary was born 30 years too soon. If she were 40 instead of 70, I am sure she would be in Congress now. She always did want to be in politics, but she was born to the farm instead. She knew all about politics and national affairs, and does plenty of first-rate thinking too. Yet she never went beyond the eighth grade in school.

George Bales drove a fractious sorrel mare, hitched to a two-wheeled racing sulky, with just a little seat on it. George began courting Mary Elizabeth by traveling over to the Taylor place, in front of which he would stop and yell till the whole Taylor household was awake; then Aunt Mary, sheepishly, would go out and join him. At first, she was a touch embarrassed to be riding around the country in a racing sulky on a tiny little seat with a man before breakfast, but she liked Uncle George, and it wasn't long at all before she looked forward to it.

And then they were married. A lot of people came over to Ernie's house that night. Ernie was now old enough and had sense enough to know that as soon as the knot was tied, the kissing would start. So he hid behind the couch.

Sure enough, as soon as the ceremony was over, Aunt Mary, crying as though she had just buried Uncle George instead of having married him, wanted to kiss everybody in the place. Especially Ernie. But Ernie couldn't be found. The search finally got so frantic and Aunt Mary made such a fuss that he decided to come out and get kissed and have it over with.

Ernie now had a new uncle, Uncle George, who lived on a farm, but wasn't a farmer. Ernie loved his Uncle George; he was a dreamer, too. He would fuss all day around his garden and his flowers, and play his beautiful big, black square piano, and order whole freight car loads of lime fertilizer he couldn't pay for. He could talk for hours about his prize sweet corn, and spend whole days studying the flower and seed catalogs he had sent away for. Uncle George was a great man, and he worked like a Trojan, but he never got anything done.

Aunt Mary had to make the living.

And she did a nice job of it, too. She raised hundreds of chickens, and she raised her own hogs and cows and she kept the treasury from going flat. She worked from four in the morning till nine at night, and found time to go to a couple of weekly women's clubs and run the country church besides.

Not only did Ernie's Aunt Mary get a husband and a 65-acre farm, she also got an unusual piano. She thoroughly appreciated her husband's musical talents and encouraged him to play for her. After a long hot day in the field, he would bathe off in a tub behind the well house, trim his moustache, put on a white shirt and then hit the keyboard! Sometimes it was difficult for Mary to get Uncle George off the black piano stool. He immersed himself in his music and became oblivious to the problems of the outside world.

There wasn't much musical talent in the Pyle family. Maria gave up playing the violin after one of the Kuhns kids told her it sounded like two cats fighting. Her knowledge of the piano was limited; she could not read music very well as was terrible accompaniment for little Ernest, who took a couple of whacks at the violin. Will Pyle could play the harmonica and the 'Jew's harp,' but his kind of music was not much in demand. The one source of refined music in the community came from the household of Tot and Harry Bales. Mariam, their only daughter and Ernie's first puppy love, became an accomplished pianist, who performed regularly in front of the local church and school gatherings.

Lots of people had pianos back in those days, but few families ever saw a Henry F. Miller square grand like the one at the Bales. Made of rosewood and glistening black lacquer, it was a quite a conversation piece. During the warm summer months, people used to drive slowly down the gravel road in their open cars, hoping to could catch some of George Bales' sophisticated music. Many young lovers used to park in their buggies west of the house, when it was a hot and humid evening, and listen to Chopin or *The Robert E. Lee* in ragtime. They would dream great dreams as the music came drifting across the cornfields.

Aunt Mary and George would grow old together. The older George Bales got, the more he played the piano. It became an obsession with him. "George Bales should have played concerts," Mary told her sister, Maria, one day. "He insists on arriving at all of our church meetings and Bill's school affairs an hour or so early," she said, "just so he could try out their piano." In fact, she said they were having a revival meeting at the Bono Methodist Church and George arrived early and started playing . . . and the preacher had to hold up the meeting from starting on time until George finished the number he was working on. He figured they needed a little culture and he didn't care if they snickered and nudged each other when the preacher got restless. "Can you imagine," marveled Aunt Mary, "a stubborn pianist!"

Aunt Mary used to joke about all of the redheads along our gravel road. Aunt Maria Pyle had red hair. Bill Bales had wavy auburn hair, his uncle Doc Sturm just down the road had red hair, as did his son, Paul Sturm, who was Ernie's age. "But Ernie's hair isn't just red," she would say, "it's something else!" It was fuzzy and kinky, kind of like a shaggy red mop. Ernie's mother didn't like it cut short like the other boys' hair. For years, Bill Bales and his new mama called Ernie "Shag" because of his red shaggy hair. Ernie visited Aunt Mary and the older Bill Bales, and, because he stood up for little Ernie when he was kidded about the red hair, whatever Bill Bales said was O.K. "Shag" was a name Ernie grew to be proud of.

One of the greatest improvements in this rural community was the arrival of the telephone lines throughout the countryside. The Pyle family got their first telephone in the spring of 1910, along with 7 other neighbors who were hooked up on what they called the "party line". The wooden telephone box was secured to the wall about head high. Will Pyle installed this wonderful contraption just inside the dining room door as you came in from the porch. It had an extended mouthpiece, which was adjustable up or down, with a crank on the right side of the box and the receiver on the left hanging in a receiver rack. This network among the neighbors became not only a means of communication, but rather a new source of entertainment.

Each household had its own call sign, which was how many short and long turns of the crank one made. Everyone knew all of the signals. The Pyle residence required three long rings, if one expected someone to answer on the other end. The Harry Bales call was two longs and a short. The George Bales home was a short and two longs. If one wished to call someone not in this network, one merely rang one short ring and "central" up in Dana would answer from the big switchboard. Then she would ring you party. The nicest part of this incredible invention was that when you cranked in a call to someone, it rang in all seven households. If one wished to listen in on a conversation between two neighbors it was simple, just pick up the receiver and listen quietly. It was not unusual for four or five neighbors to be listening in on one call. It provided a lot of entertainment and information. When a curious neighbor picked up to "listen in" as it was called, one could hear a little click of the interruption on the line.

By the age of 10, Ernest was working daily during the summertime with his father who tried to teach him the art of carpentry, the technique of painting dry wood siding with white lead and linseed oil, the procedures for planting and harvesting the crops, and the skills needed to prepare for the cold winter months.

Ernest recorded his humble savings in his ledger book. He kept his money in a cigar box in his dresser drawer, and it had grown into a sizeable fortune for a boy his age. His mother often spoke of college. She would discuss the schools the neighboring boys and girls planned to attend. But it was obvious that Ernest was not interested in becoming a teacher and going to Indiana State in Terre Haute. The walls of his small west bedroom were pasted heavily with cutouts of racing cars, speedboats, motorcycles, racehorses, and anything else that was a high-speed conveyance. The walls seemed to say, "Ernest may not know where he's going, but wherever he does go, he's going to go there fast."

Chapter 8

A Member of the Community

On a cold winter afternoon in January 1913, Aunt Mary dropped by the Taylor place for a visit. Now that her father, Lambert Taylor, had passed on and John, her brother, had his own home with a growing family, Aunt Mary often felt obliged to check in on Maria and her family. Will was out in the field finishing up his chores. He'd finally gotten around to removing several old hickory stumps from an overgrown corner of the property that needed tending to. Maria had just left to take Lelia Kuhns a custard pie she had baked to thank her for helping with a recent church social.

Aunt Mary knocked on the front door. When no one answered, she hollered "you-hoo" a couple of times. She decided she was being foolish standing outside in the freezing cold as if she had never lived there a day in her life! No one locked their doors in Helt Township, and she felt perfectly comfortable letting herself in. She was pleased to find her old home warm and cozy, but she was, however, startled to see Shep, Ernie's favorite dog, buried deep under quilted covers — asleep with little Ernest on the couch no less! Shep was definitely not a housedog, but, then she remembered, it was often acceptable for dogs to come inside during sub-zero weather. Ernie must've gotten a dispensation from his mama for Shep to come. It was very cold this after-noon.

"Oh, hi, Aunt Mary," yawned Ernie, now 12 years old, as he and Shep awoke and scrambled off the couch onto the floor, "winter gets so lonely around here all I want to do is nap." Ernie was an only child, and even though he had many friends, it was sometimes hard to find things to do on such miserable days. Aunt Mary sat down in her favorite chair and observed Ernie and Shep. They both crawled over to the rug lying close to the baseburner stove. "If I didn't have Shep, I don't know what I'd do," he con-tinued. "I reckon I'd just about go crazy." He patted Shep's head and then hugged him tightly.

The cold winter isolation of farm life in Indiana was, for Ernie, all the more dismal because his mother and dad were so much older than the parents of the other kids his age. *Mama and Papa aren't nearly as fun*, may have been what he was thinking, but what he said to his Aunt Mary was, "It sure would be great to have a brother or a sister to play with."

"Of course it would, Ernest," she said, "but you can always play with the Kuhns kids or Thad or with George Potter. And don't forget Shep!" Shep was a "country-style" American shepherd, a shepherd, that is, that quite likely has a few other varieties mixed in. But Shep was Ernie's best friend, especially during the long winter months when he was housebound. He was thankful to have such a good dog to love.

Ernie beamed, "If there is a human being in this world who is kinder, more understanding, more faithful, or more intelligent than this dog, then I sure want to know him." Shep was his constant companion. In the entire vast prairie there was not a soul who understood Ernie's mind better than Shep. When Ernie's feelings were hurt, he would sometimes go out into the yard and lie down and cry. Sure enough, Shep would come and lie beside him, and lick his face and whine in a complete and understanding sympathy. Ernie sure did love Shep.

"Aunt Mary, my friend George Potter's dog was killed a few summers ago. He had a real hard time talking about it," Ernie said. "I don't know how I would feel if I lost Shep." They were curled up together on the floor and Ernie was still scratching behind Shep's ears. Every now and then Ernie would scratch just the right spot and then Shep's leg would start pounding like a motor on all cylinders. As far as Ernie was concerned, the greatest shepherd dog that ever lived was right there in a humble household on an Indiana farm.

"Ernie, we all have to let go of things we love at different times in life. You know, your Uncle George lost his first wife, and it took a long while for him and for Bill to get through the hurt. But he did, and I'm happy he did. He found me," she smiled. Aunt Mary always had the right words to make Ernie feel good.

And Ernie was happy for Aunt Mary, too.

"George Potter said he thought he knew who shot his dog," Ernie said, not voicing the local suspicion that it was Sam Elder. "What could make a man kill a dog," asked Ernie with a genuinely puzzled and confused look on his freckled face.

Aunt Mary knew most of what went for gossip in her neighborhood. Ernie's mama had shared the story about the Potter boy's dog, and Aunt Mary was well aware that the neighborhood boys were convinced it was Sam Elder who had killed the dog. Most grownups knew that Sam Elder was within his rights but that he should've known the dog wasn't a sheep killer. "I don't know, Ernie, I just don't know," said Aunt Mary as Ernie tenderly stroked Shep's coat. "Some people are just not that considerate and understanding of the feelings of others. They're just mean-spirited."

After a few moments, Aunt Mary continued, "You won't remember this, but you know you were born over at Sam Elder's place in that little tenant shack. You lived there for about three months after you were born. Well, Ernie, Sam Elder sometimes treated your mom and dad like he owned them. He didn't actually believe he owned them, it's just that he treated them as if he did. And that's the point, Ernie. There are people in the world like Sam who just don't seem to have learned that that there's no difference between believin' and treatin'."

Cold winter winds made the recent arrival of telephone lines hum and sing like banjo strings. The trees would snap and crackle. One's breath looked like a steam vent blowing against the numbing cold. Papers and rags were stuffed around the window sash to keep out the drifting snow. The watering troughs froze solid. Fruit jars would sometimes burst open in the pantry. Even the lantern was left burning for what little heat it could produce.

January, February, and March were torturous months. The Canadian cold fronts swept across this part of the Midwest like blizzards from the Yukon, leaving in their paths 20-degrees-below-zero weather. When there was snow on the ground, the wild birds and animals often starved for lack of food or just froze solid in the sustained blast of arctic air; no snow and the ground froze as hard as granite, making it difficult to walk and care for the livestock.

But one thing was always for certain. The crow flights never ceased! Starting at daybreak, a flying river of black crows would appear from the west, gliding quietly with the wind, on their migration to the Wabash Valley area in search of food. Corn that had been overlooked by the shuckers, was their staple diet. In the evening this endless line of crows would start its trek to the osage hedgerows of eastern Illinois where the flock by the thousands would noisily bed down for a freezing night. Flying into the cold, penetrating winds on the trip west was a tiring and difficult flight. This black ribbon of crows often would stretch for miles, and added a sense of sadness or bleakness to an otherwise happy community.

One of the great luxuries of that time was the base-burner, a beautiful, heavy stove loaded with chrome and ironwork and isinglass windows. Will and Maria Pyle bought a baseburner that lasted for years and was a modern miracle for producing heat. Most of their neighbors bought the same make and model, the "Round Oak Base Burner," sold at the H. L. Fillinger hardware store in Dana. In the dead of winter, these glowing, smokeless stoves warmed many a cold mitten and chilled foot throughout the county.

The baseburner used either coke or hard coal, and burned

continuously just as long as the hamper was filled. Coke was the preferred fuel because it burned cleanly and gave off little if any smoke. Coke is coal that has had its more volatile chemical impurities removed. The baseburner's hamper was filled from the top, so it took a pretty strong person to swing the top of the stove around and pour in a bucket of the coke.

In the Pyle home, the baseburner was in the living room just outside of Will and Maria's bedroom. It was always a welcome sight to see the big, reliable stove casting forth its red glow on a cold wintry night. As long as there was coke or hard coal in the woodshed, there would be a fire burning in the baseburner, but if the fire burned out, restarting it was a family chore that usually landed on Ernie's shoulders now that he was getting older.

First, all of the ashes and clinkers had to be removed, which meant the grates had to be "shaken down" using the attachable handle. Once the grates were cleaned, the ashes and clinkers removed, and the ash pan in place, Ernie would then carefully stack dried corncobs, bits of kindling, and even a few pieces of coke inside the bowl of the burner. He would then sprinkle the cobs with oil and finally throw in a lighted match.

When this blazing mixture of kindling, cobs, and coal was producing sufficient heat, Ernie would place grey pieces of coke into the inferno. Getting the coke to "catch on" was a feat of engineering. Once a few pieces caught on and started turning pink, more pieces were carefully added to the fire. Gradually, more and more of the hard coke started burning. Then came the final test. When the fire was burning properly, an entire bucket of coke was poured in from the top of the stove, completely smothering any sign of the burning coals underneath. The first sign of success was a thread of blue-pink flame emerging from the grey heap of coke. Then came the sharp crackle that told you the fire was smoldering deep beneath the pile. In a few hours, the baseburner was churning out the heat and again warming a cold, cold house.

Spring arrived but was quickly forgotten as the quiet, uneventful summer of 1913 loped along in its lazy pace towards Ernie's thirteenth birthday. And the pace was just a little too lazy as far as the young Ernie Pyle was concerned. In a few weeks he would turn thirteen. When a farm boy turns thirteen he is expected to work in the field, and Ernie was so eager to join the men in this year's threshing circle that he had thought of very little else since the first blossoms appeared on the apple trees in late April. It seemed that every one of his friends were in the same state of suspended animation, all anticipating this year's harvest time. He and Thad Hooker had only been riding twice!

Ernest Taylor Pyle had spent a restless mid-July night filled with wild dreams and anxious thoughts. Tomorrow was the day he would start to work with the grown men. He would turn thirteen years old in a few weeks, and he fully intended to look and do his part when his time came. He wanted to be accepted. He was going to *earn* his 50-cents-a-day. In the meantime, he was getting a head start by helping a little early with the cutting and the shocking.

"Ernest, get up now. I've called you twice already."

"But, Mama, couldn't I sleep just a little longer? It's dark outside," replied a sleepy little boy. He was still curled up in the corner of his three-quarter-sized iron bed.

"It's almost 4:30, Ernest. Your papa has already gone up to the barn. You're gonna be a paid man soon, so get on up!" directed a stern but loving mother. She and Will wanted to give their little boy an early enough start so he could have time to adjust to his new responsibilities. Although he wouldn't actually be doing much in the field today, she wanted to make sure Ernest would have a head start. She was worried that he might have trouble blending into the rough-and-ready work force of seasoned harvesters.

"All right, mama, I'm gettin' up. I can smell the coffee."

It had been a good year for the crops, especially the oats. Will Pyle had sowed 20 acres of oats in the field to the west of the house and it was an especially good crop.

"It may make 40 bushels an acre, Maria," Will had told his wife a few Sundays before, in early July. Will and Maria were on their way to visit Mary and George Bales and had driven by the field in their buggy.

"Oh, I hope so, Will," Maria had said. "If the price holds up we could make enough to build a new chicken house." Maria's mind was always at work. After all, the Mound was not blessed with the rich, black land of the farms to their immediate west. The Pyle's earth was a hardscrabble mix of clay and yellow soil, and Maria and Will had accepted that they would have to work harder than most to produce a living. Maria was always trying to come up with new ways to make their 77 acres more efficient and productive.

Farming was a neighborhood effort, and no farmer in the community need be short of help or equipment. Will Pyle had asked Claude Lockridge to cut the Pyle oat crop when it was ready. Now, a few weeks before Ernie's thirteenth birthday on August 3rd, Claude, with Will Pyle's help, pulled his binder into the driveway with four strong and sweaty horses. Ernie had just finished his breakfast and had come out to join them, ready for whatever may come. Although he had seen a binder many times, now that he was up close and it had his full attention he was stunned to see how big it really was. It had been designed so it could be pulled down the road end-ways, which was its narrowest part, to allow for easy transport.

Claude Lockridge was a good engineer; he knew exactly what he was doing. He pulled the binder right to the edge of the ripe oat field and climbed down from the driver's seat. As Ernie looked on, Claude and Will started converting the binder into a harvesting machine, which meant changing the tongue from the front end to the side. Ernie marveled at this incredible machine. Simply by adjusting the wheels and changing the binder tongue with the doubletrees, the horses could pull it sideways so that its sharp sickle could scissor cut the dry stalks. It would rumble across the hot, yellow fields of ripe grain leaving a swathe of stubble, littered with neatly tied sheaves.

"Here comes Bill Bales now," said Will Pyle as he was tightening up the canvas conveyor belt on the binder.

"Is he going to help us shock, Will?" asked Claude.

"Sure is; George said we could use him because they've already finished their wheat," said Will. "You know George only put out 10 acres this year."

"I hear he's now into soy beans," said Claude.

"He's trying 'em out. Says it'll be the crop of the future someday," added Will, shaking his head in wonder. "Ain't that just like George. Always trying something different."

"He and Mary sure work hard on that place," continued Claude. "Mary did real well on her chickens this year, didn't she?"

"Yup, Mary kind'a keeps things going," said Will, as he continued to work on converting the binder. He knew Mary more like a sister than a sister-in-law. Mary's constant fuss to take control of most matters around the house always tickled him. "I'm having trouble getting these belts tight enough, Claude."

"Wait for Bill. He can fix it," Claude said. "Bill sure is a big fella for a 20-year-old, isn't he? Must weigh 225 pounds." Claude and Will watched Bill as he was heading to put his mare away. "He'll be back in a few minutes to help us."

Bill Bales had grown into a big, rough farmer always willing to help out if his father wasn't using him. Not only had he acquired a new mother when Mary Taylor married his widowed father, he had also become part of the Pyle family; Ernie was like his little brother and Maria and Will were now as much kinfolk as a true aunt and uncle. He spent a lot of time at the Pyle house.

Claude completed the final check of the rollers, tarps, sprockets, cogs, wheels, and levers. He backed his four big horses into position in front of the binder.

"You got enough binder twine, Will?" asked Claude as he started snapping the tugs to the singletrees.

"Maria bought four new rolls when we were in town Saturday. I think we have enough."

The farmers who were fortunate enough to own such binders would harvest their neighbors grain for a reasonable fee, usually taken out in a wagonload or two of the threshed crop. No one was in a particular hurry to be paid off; everyone had confidence that after the harvest was over, there would be enough money to settle all debts and obligations.

Today, Will and his young help, Bill Bales, were going to shock the oats, while Claude would keep the binder in operation. Carefully, Claude adjusted the harness on his horses and checked the reins before he climbed up on the iron seat, where he could survey the whole operation from a position of command.

"I'm going to open up the field, Will. You and Bill follow me around," instructed Claude. He looked to the east at the fast climbing sun. It was going to be one of those hot, dry July days with no rain in sight.

Bill Bales wiped his broad forehead with his red bandana.

"Do you reckon we can get this cut and shocked today, Claude?"

"We should make it before dark if nothing breaks down. I had some trouble with it yesterday, but Charlie Cooper came by last night and fixed it. The binder twine was breaking every time it tied. Hope it works all right today," he grumbled as he leaned over the seat and unloaded a big gob of chewin' tobacco on the hard ground.

"Giddyap, let's go," snapped Claude to the team of horses. They immediately lurched in the harness. There was a great cloud of dust and a terrific clatter of wheels. Sprockets and gears groaned as the McCormick binder took its first big bite of Will Pyle's oat field at 7:40 a.m. on a hot July morning in 1913.

Claude "opened" the field by circling Will Pyle's 20 acres clockwise, with the horses walking in the uncut grain while the binder kicked out sheaves of newly cut oats into the fence row. Once this was done, Claude reversed the pattern and began the tedious job of creating ever-diminishing circles, which finally produced a barren stubble field littered with hundreds of sheaves of golden oats.

Will Pyle and Bill Bales followed close behind the binder, stacking the sheaves of oats into carefully designed shocks. First they would stand two sheaves together with the butt ends jabbed solidly into the stubble. Around these two, they would stack another dozen sheaves until they had a round stack of ripe oats with the heads glistening in the heavy heat. As a final touch to the design, one last sheaf was picked up, broken in the middle by spreading out the grain end of the sheaf, and placed as a cap on top of the shock. Carefully, the cap was placed so the heads on the oats were toward the northwest. Most of the thunderstorms came from the northwest, and once the shock settled, even the strongest wind couldn't dislodge the cap. It covered the top and reminded Ernie of a mother hen protecting her brood.

The air was still and the July heat was on top of them like an iron lid on a skillet. Maria Pyle shuttled Ernest back and forth from the field. Ernest not only had water duty, he had the intermittent responsibility of helping his mother prepare the dinner. They had extra mouths to feed and she needed help in preparations. At noon, Maria sent Ernie back out to the field to call the men in for dinner. After washing their arms and faces in the big pans of cool water that Ernie had filled and set out by the well, William Pyle, Claude Lockridge, and big Bill Bales were ready for Maria's fried chicken, iced tea, fresh green beans, mashed potatoes, and biscuits.

The men wasted little time in digging in. They were anxious to get back to the partially harvested field of oats and get the job done before darkness set in.

"Ernie," Bill Bales said to Ernie, as he cleaned off his plate and took a bite of fresh apple pie baked that morning by Maria, "your dad tells me that he is going to hire you to be the water boy in the threshing ring this year."

"Yeh, Bill, Papa says I may get the job, but I need a better buggy. Could I use yours?" asked the eager Ernest, obviously excited about his first grownup job for pay.

"Sure, Shag, when you get ready, come over and pick up my buggy. Its gotta new top on it. You'll like the shade while you're in the fields," replied Bill. Bill always looked after Ernie and Ernie liked the nickname "Shag" that Bill had been given him. "Guess we'd better get back to cuttin' oats."

Ernie hitched up his overall suspenders and followed big Bill Bales out on the porch, clearly in awe of his big, kind step-cousin, who had arms as big as fence posts. Ernie was thankful that he had an older buddy like Bill; it put a stop to all of the kidding he got at school for being so skinny and puny.

"You men get on back to the field. You're going to have

to hurry to finish up by evening," fussed Maria. She glanced at the thermometer hanging on the side of the porch. "It's 92 right now. I'll have Ernest bring out a jug of cold water this afternoon. He and Paul are going to try and get me a rabbit when you get near the end of the cutting." Young, fried rabbit was considered a delicacy this time of year. During the late summer evenings, the young rabbits would play in the dust along the gravel roads, darting in and out of the heavy grass and weed converge of the ditches.

Bill Bales turned towards the kitchen door, where Ernie's mama was standing, "Thanks, Maria. That apple pie was just what I needed," responded Claude. He pulled his tattered straw hat down over his sunburned face and plucked a goose quill out of his shirt pocket and started picking his teeth.

"Well, we'll never get done standing here in the shade," chuckled Will Pyle. His sun bleached blue shirt and pants were ringed with white sweat marks from the heat. Shocking oats was a hot and dirty job.

The three men and the four horses went back to the west field and soon had the binder and its revolving reaper churning through the oat field under the blazing afternoon sun. Sweat dripped from their chins as they kept circling the field, each time in a smaller circle.

"It must be about five, Claude," said Will later that afternoon as the binder paused to negotiate a tight turn at the corner. The horses were lathered white with sweat. Around the horse collars were sweat marks from the heat and flies.

Will Pyle and Bill Bales were "keeping up" with the binder and had left several hundred shocks of oats in a symmetrical pattern around the field. Their blue work shirts were wet with perspiration. Another couple of hours and they would have their day's work done.

"Here comes Ernest and Paul with some water," said Will, glancing toward the Pyle house. Ernie had asked his next-door neighbor, Paul Sturm, to come by in the afternoon, when the binder would almost be through cutting. While Ernest would be 13 years old in about three weeks, Paul had already had his 13th birthday in May. Although Ernest and Paul were born the same year, there was a considerable difference in size. Paul was unusually tall for his age, whereas Ernie weighed only 68 pounds. Both boys had red wavy hair under their straw hats, and each carried a broomstick over his shoulder. They were after big game this time!

Chasing rabbits was a common sport at the end of cutting a field of grain. The time for chasing rabbits caught up in the process was right when the binder had reduced the size of the oat field to the point where the rabbits could no longer scurry to shelter. A shortened broomstick, about three feet long, was the weapon of choice to chase the fleeing young rabbits. If the rabbits were grown, they had a good chance to outdistance their pursuers, but since the younger rabbits got confused, there were good odds that a thrown broomstick would hit its mark.

"You boys follow the binder over there on the other side of the patch of oats. If there are any rabbits in there, they are going to come running out the other side. I'll yell if I see one from up here," said Claude with a grin on his face.

The four big horses and the clattering binder gradually reduced the uncut strip of the field to a narrow parcel of standing grain. Each time the noisy binder made its round, the anxiety increased for the two big game hunters. It was hot and dusty, and the stubble stuck into their legs, but Ernest and Paul kept a patient vigil on the lookout for fleeing rabbits.

"There goes one!" yelled Claude as he pulled his team of tired horses to a stop.

"I see him!" yelled Ernest, running along the edge of the uncut oats. "He's gone back in the oats!"

The tension mounted. The two farm boys armed with broomsticks, waited for their prey to be exposed in the open stubble field. Once all of the grain was finished being cut, there would be no place for the rabbits to hide.

"Over here, over here!" yelled Will Pyle from the far end of the field, pointing to a bouncing cottontail headed for the Campbell's pasture just to the west.

"I see him!" yelled Paul, whose long legs carried him ahead of Ernest. Both boys were in hot pursuit, and rapidly gaining on the young rabbit.

Claude, Will, and Bill all stopped to observe the chase. The rabbit now was only 50 yards from freedom, if it could reach the rail fence in time.

Ernest yelled to Paul, "Throw at him, Paul!"

Paul swung his broomstick around his head and let go. The three-foot broom handle went whistling through the air, end over end, toward the fleeing cottontail. The rabbit suddenly dodged to the right and ran parallel to the fence for a few long leaps. Next, Ernie's broomstick came sailing over the rabbit's head. In a quick change of pace, the rabbit made a left-hand turn, zipped under the rail fence, and was on his merry way to Harry Bales' apple orchard.

"You let him get away, Shag," yelled Bill Bales. He had been watching the whole spectacle from the other side of the field. "Now you won't have rabbit for supper."

"He was too fast for us. We came close, though, didn't we, Paul?" Ernie said, obviously disappointed.

"You boys just didn't run fast enough," kidded Claude. He then flicked his horses on the rumps with the lines and turned the binder for another run. Another half-hour should do it — quittin' time soon.

"Papa, you know it was a big rabbit, almost full grown," Ernest pleaded, as his father walked over to speak to them.

"Don't worry, Ernest, that rabbit just wasn't meant to be eaten," chuckled Will Pyle with a sparkle in his eyes. "You and Paul scared him, though, and that's for sure,"

Paul retrieved his broomstick. "I'm goin' home through the woods," Paul yelled back to Ernest, using the broom handle like a sword. "Maybe I'll meet up with King Arthur or Little John down there by the creek." The tall lanky boy jumped the rail fence and crossed the road into the Sturm's woods. He waved goodbye and faded away through the trees.

It had been a long, hard day for the Pyle family. They now had their oat crop cut and safely shocked and now they would await threshing time, which would arrive in about two or three weeks, once the oats had dried out. The weather promised not to vex their efforts; it was unlikely that a heavy rain or windstorm would threaten the crop.

That evening, during supper, Ernest told his mother how close he came to getting a young rabbit for her big, black, cast-iron skillet.

"Ernest, you can't catch 'em all," mused his mother. "Life just isn't that way. You and Paul must have given him a good chase; your father said you almost got him. There'll be other times." After a moment, she added, "Maybe you can catch him in your trap this winter. He'll be just as good eating then."

The next three weeks passed much too slowly for Ernie. When August 3rd finally arrived, Aunt Mary and Uncle George came over for supper and brought a freezer of newly made ice cream. Aunt Mary had sent Uncle George to town in his iron-wheeled wagon, pulled by "Sam and Jack," two big, stalwart mules, to fetch a 100-pound block of ice from White's Ice House on Front Street. During the hot summer months, the icehouse produced five tons of ice daily for the community!

For his birthday, Ernie's mother gave him a new blue work shirt with a small leather accounting book in which he could keep a record of his earnings. His father gave him a new pair of knob-toed work shoes that came up ankle high. Aunt Mary and Uncle George gave him two 50-cent pieces as starter cash for his bank account.

Since the lingering death of Lambert Taylor in the spring of last year, 1911, the Pyle household had been reorganized. Maria and Will now had Taylor's bedroom. Their former bedroom, next to Ernest's, had been made into a sitting room. Ernest kept his bedroom in the northwest corner of the house. He was thankful that he could sleep with the window wide open now that his father had made screens for the west window. It got so hot during harvest time!

As was the custom for organizing a harvest circle, a group of neighbors meet and decide just what each was to furnish to make the threshing ring complete. This year, the black steam engine and the thresher would be furnished by Jump Houchin. Doc Sturm would furnish a hayrack and a team of horses. Harry Bales volunteered his grain wagon and a team, as did George Bales. Claude Lockridge would bring a team and a hayrack, as would Silas Jones. Since Frank Kuhns had more acreage than the others, he would furnish a hayrack and a team and also a grain wagon. The pitchers, who employed a three-tined, long-handled pitchfork for tossing the sheaves up to the man on the wagon rack, would be Will Pyle, Oat Saxton, Bill Bales, Sam Saxton and Howard Goforth, hired by Doc Sturm.

The water boy, who was expected to furnish his own horse, buggy, and water jugs, would be Ernest Taylor Pyle. His first job with the grown men was soon to arrive!! The agreed price was 50 cents a day. This was an important and never ending job during threshing time. It would take lots of fresh water to quench the thirst of the field workers.

"Ernest, you get ready for your breakfast right quick. I've got hot biscuits in the oven and some fresh raspberry jam for you, so hurry up! Your papa will be in from the barn with the milk soon, and he'll want to eat and get on the way to Harry's. You need to be in the field by 7:30."

"All right, Mama. I've got my jugs all lined up by the well. I'll fill 'em as soon as I eat. Then I'll hitch up and go; Papa's riding with me."

"He's got your mare all hitched up for you. Now you remember, Ernest, those men expect cold drinking water, so you come in and get fresh water every time you get a chance. Harry will want you to use the well there by the gate. Be careful of the jugs; they belong to the neighbors. I put clean cobs in two of them and aired them out yesterday."

"Thanks, Mama. I'll be real careful. I can do it. I'll eat when Papa eats. I guess they'll start in the north field first."

Ernest Taylor Pyle set off hurriedly that hot August morning sitting on top of the world. He was the envy of the boys in the neighborhood as he had a responsible job that paid money.

Will Pyle helped his son load the five water jugs in the back of the buggy and then swung himself up into the seat. Waving goodbye to Maria, the father and son set off down the gravel road.

"Now, Ernest, don't get too close to the threshing machine, it might drag you in. Wear your straw hat as it is going to be real hot today," yelled Maria, giving one last word of advice to her only son.

Each day dragged on like a week to Ernest. He and Cricket, his mare, made a dozen trips daily in the buggy. They would travel from the well to the field, where he delivered fresh water to the harvest workers, and back again. At the well, he would empty each jug and fill it with fresh water, then seal it by jamming a corncob into the neck of the jug. He got used to the routine and looked forward each day to a new experience. He had earned his first title — he was a full-fledged "Water Boy." He learned that some of the workers used two hands while drinking from the jug, while others preferred the fancy one-hand-over-the-forearm method of wetting their whistles. The days were hot, but since everyone else was working in the August heat, Ernest never seemed to mind the thermometer readings, which were a subject of constant conversation.

The most exciting part of the thresher's day was the noontime meal, always called "dinner." At high noon, a dinner bell was sounded as the signal for everyone to taper off and get ready for dinner. The sound of the big iron bell, mounted on a post in the backyard, brought smiles to the dirty and sweaty faces out in the harvest field. Even the horses responded to the sound. They got a rest and a good serving of oats and corn, too.

It was the custom for the wives to help with the dinner. These "thresher dinners" became events in and of themselves, subjects of animated conversation throughout the long winter months to come. Nothing was too good for the harvesters, and the wives saw to it that nothing was spared from their gastrointestinal desires. Each harvest dinner was quite an experience, with many desserts thrown in. All the wives looked forward to the day that this same crew would work at their farm, so they would have the occasion to display fancy cooking to the men folk of the neighborhood.

On the eighth day of the harvest, the threshers started working at the Pyle oat field. Will had marked a place near the log barn where he wanted the new straw pile, so Mr. Houchin spotted the big separator in place with its long metal stack pointed at the future haystack. He then backed the large, black steam engine into place about 60 feet away from the separator and lined it up with his sharp eye. He carefully rolled out a very long, four-inch wide, leather belt, which was over 100 feet in length. He looped it over the flywheel of the engine and over the main pulley of the thresher. The belt was given a half twist to keep it rotating in place. He carefully inched the large-wheeled, coal-burning engine back a few feet until he had the exact right tension in the belt. Reaching up above the cab, Mr. Houchin gave the whistle cord a couple of quick jerks, signaling that he was ready to take the first load of sheaved oats from the heavily loaded hayrack standing by.

While the men were bringing in the shocked oats to the thresher, the women were all scurrying around the Pyle house preparing a dinner fit for a king.

Carrie Sturm had brought two cakes, Tot Bales had cut up fried chicken, Mary Bales was cranking the last turns on her ice cream freezer, Lelia Kuhns brought egg noodles and a bowl of banana pudding, Lou Lockridge brought a big pan of light bread dough, which would be rolled out and shaped into rolls and loaves. Violet Jones had made a fresh peach cobbler, and Juanita Saxton brought a large bowl of slaw. It was going to be a feast!

"Mary, there are flies there in the dining room. Get a dish towel and let's shoo them out before the other girls get here," said

Maria as she surveyed the dining room table she had been setting with her odd assortment of china. She had ironed the large, white tablecloth the night before.

"They are always worse at harvest time, Maria. Here, you start in that corner and I'll prop the front door open so we can shoo them out," replied Mary who had arrived at 6 a.m. to help her sister put on the threshers dinner. By flapping dishtowels, made from Pillsbury flour sacks, in front of them, Maria and Mary scared the flies off the ceiling and directed them to the open front door where they could retreat in full flight.

"Maria, it's almost noon. Can I ring the bell now?" asked Lelia Kuhns, the Pyle's next door neighbor.

"Yes, I think it's about time. It looks like we have everything ready. Lu, how about your rolls — are they ready to be put in yet?"

"No, I want them to rise a little higher; but go ahead, the men won't be ready to eat yet for another 20 minutes or so."

The cast-iron, coal range in the Pyle kitchen had been radiating heat and belching smoke all morning long until the little kitchen felt like an oven itself. There was gravy to be made, chicken to fry, potatoes to mash, noodles to be boiled, sweet potatoes to be candied, and, all the while, the oven was accommodating a yellow cake and two gooseberry pies. The rolls had to get in there someplace — it just took timing and Maria knew just how to orchestrate this operation!

The workers came to the house wet with sweat and itching from chafe and dust. Their first stop was out by the well where they stripped their shirts off and plunged their heads into tubs of cool water that had already been prepared for them. The yellow lye soap and cool water made them feel clean again. It felt good to "freshen up" and get away from the oat chaff and the stubble for an hour.

Adding two extra table leaves had stretched the small dining-room table. Now, eleven empty chairs plus the piano stool surrounded the heavy-laden oak table. There wasn't even room for the bouquet of zinnias Aunt Mary had brought from her garden. Every available space on the table was covered with chinaware, dishes, crocks, plates, water glasses, and platters.

Only the workingmen sat at the table, where the wives and children would dutifully wait upon their every request. After some good-natured jostling and scraping of chairs, the entire threshing team pulled themselves up to the table. Complete silence followed as every head bowed.

"Our most gracious Heavenly Father, we thank Thee for the blessings of this harvest time. We thank Thee for the opportunity to serve Thee, and pray that Thou will watch over those who are harvesting Thy grain.

"We thank Thee for our friends and neighbors who are with us today, and we ask a special prayer of Thee, our Heavenly Father, that you will be with Elnora Potter who has been poorly this summer.

"We ask that Thou will bless this food to our bodies and those who have prepared it, for we ask this in the name of Jesus Christ, Our Lord. Amen," spoke Will Pyle in a soft and gentle voice.

No sooner had the last words fallen than the table became a blur of long arms reaching and passing food.

"Claude, you'd better take two pieces of chicken," Tot Bales said as she passed a large platter full of hot fried chicken across the table between Claude and Bill Bales.

"Tot, don't try to feed those two guys. They'll eat everything on the table. Save something for the rest of us!" chuckled Harry Bales who was a good-natured kidder, and never short of words. Mariam, his 12-year-old daughter, was helping to serve the table.

"Daddy," she said. "You eat more than my pony!"

"Well, if I have to work like a horse, I might as well eat like one," said Harry, as the table laughed. He spooned out a generous helping of hot egg noodles and fresh cabbage slaw on his plate.

The Pyle dinner this hot day in August, 1913, consisted of the following: Fried chicken, baked hen and noodles, fried ham, mashed potatoes, candied sweet potatoes, fresh green beans with sow belly, chicken gravy, ham gravy, baked beans, Cole slaw, sliced tomatoes, sliced onions, fresh corn cut off the cob and fried in bacon drippings, creamed pearl onions, fresh lima beans, cucumber salad, fresh baby beets and potato salad, fresh cottage cheese served with extra cream and lots of salt and pepper, followed by such desserts as cool watermelon (which had been floating in the horse tank), fresh peach cobbler, green harvest apple pie, vinegar pie, banana pudding and a freezer of homemade ice cream. There was coffee and iced tea flavored with fresh mint from the creek down in Mr. Webster's pasture. An assortment of the best of jams and jellies were on the table served right out of the jar. These included black raspberry jelly, currant and apple jelly, watermelon rind preserves, blackberry jam and some fresh pear preserves made the day before by Mary Bales.

"Come on, men," cackled Oat Saxton. "It's time to break up this feast - we won't be able to work if we eat any more!"

"Just save some for supper," said George Bales who preferred a heavy meal after he had finished all of his evening chores at the barn.

"Pass me some more of that chicken gravy, Oat," asked John Sturm.

Oat Saxton, always a happy and jovial man was the storyteller of the neighborhood. His stories were fictitious and made up about colorful local people. Every boy in the countryside loved to hear Oat Saxton spin his yarns about the neighbors. His laughter would ring from the rafters as he laughed harder than anyone at his own stories.

A thresher's dinner was always one of abundance of both good food and lots of shady jokes, and many belly laughs. The Pyle dinner was no exception.

Slowly, the overstuffed farmers pulled away from the table. "By the time the kids get their dinners, there won't be a scrap left," chuckled Will Pyle as he winked at his niece, Juanita. The farmers started heading their way back to their threshing chores.

"That was a real good dinner, Maria," thanked Bill Bales, who always claimed the record for the number of light rolls consumed during a meal at the Pyle home.

"I hope you boys get done before too late."

"Oh, we're going to finish up this afternoon, then we'll pull over to Frank's this evening so we can get an early start there tomorrow," said Jump Houchin. He pulled at his galluses and adjusted the seat of his overalls.

Eight wagonloads of oats were hauled to the Dana elevator this day in August, and five more shoveled into the corner of the log barn for feed. The Pyle harvest of oats had made over 45 bushels an acre! Maria and Will figured they would clear close to $200 on this year's oat crop, which would more than pay for the materials for the new hen house. The remnants of the day were displayed in a 20-foot-tall straw pile by the barn, which would be consumed by the Pyle livestock during the long winter months.

After the thresher's circle was complete for the season, the farmers met one evening at the home of Dr. and Mrs. John Sturm, where they balanced out their obligations and paid off all of their debts. It was a community of farming at its best. Ernest

Pyle, the water boy for this eleven and a half-day harvest received the tidy sum of $5.50 for his wages.

That night, when he and his father got home from the Sturm's house, he laid the five crumpled one-dollar bills and the 50 cents out on the kitchen table to show to his mother.

"Look at it, Mama, this is all mine."

"I'm real proud of you, Ernest. Your papa wants you to put this down in your record book to show where you worked and when. You should always keep a record of your money; you'll learn to save this way and know how much to give the church. Fifty-five cents of your wages go to the Lord," said Maria Pyle, proud of her son's first take home wages.

"Yes, Mama, I'll put it in Sunday when we go to church."

Chapter 9

Someday, They'll Know My Name

Over the next year, Ernest Taylor Pyle, grew out of his boyhood. Although he remained short and wiry, he was nevertheless beginning to look more like the Taylor side of the family. His nose looked more and more like that of his grandfather, Lambert Taylor, and the red hair became curlier and fuzzier. Sitting in church on hard wooden benches through long sermons was not exactly what a teenaged farm boy looked forward to on Sunday. After all, there were horses, friends and, now, newly discovered girls to occupy one's time and thoughts!

The Pyles were staunch and faithful Methodists. They never missed a Sunday service unless the weather was too bad, or there was sickness in the family. It was a good three-mile buggy ride to the church, which sat proudly on the southwest corner of the main intersection in Bono, under two tall pine trees. Bono, a thriving farm community of maybe 100 people, had no real boundaries, but, rather, scattered out through the countryside.

The only church in the community of Bono was the little Methodist church built in 1877. It would seat up to 160 people and boasted of one of the best-tuned upright pianos in the community. It was a working church; it had to be in order to survive. Bono people were fine and proud families. The people in Dana, just three miles to the north, had six churches. Many of the neighbors and friends of the Pyle family, such as the Sturms, the Jordans, and the Bales, all of whom were members of the Methodist Church in Dana, had attended this church on the day of Maria and Will's wedding in 1899. The Pyles and their neighbors, all God-fearing and Bible-toting people, had a strong Christian bond among them.

Will and Maria Pyle gave their son a maximum of exposure to the teachings of the Good Book. They had raised an honest and upright farm boy of the highest ideals, and, now that he was thirteen, it was time he joined the church. Each spring the Bono Church had a revival meeting. New members would come down the aisle when the invitational hymn was sung. Reverend Charles Beebe held the revival in February of 1914. It was a four-night affair, Tuesday through Friday, with services starting at 7 p.m. and ending by 8:30. Seldom did the Pyles get home before 10 p.m., which didn't give Ernest much time for rest after helping his father put away the buggy and the horse.

The church wasn't very crowded on Thursday night. Although it was generally considered that Reverend Beebe improved with the size of the crowd, he nonetheless could deliver a rousing sermon on most every occasion. Ernest was flanked on either side by his mother and father, and he felt very uneasy that night. The preacher stressed the ravages of life in hell for all sinners.

"Dost thou renounce the devil and all of his works, the vain pomp and glory of the world, with all covetous desires of the same, and the carnal desires of the flesh, so that thou wilt not follow nor be led by them?" boomed the preacher in his thunderous voice. "The only way to be saved is to give one's life to Christ and be baptized into the church with the Holy Trinity." Ernest wasn't sure just what all of this meant, but his mother kept nodding reassuringly that this was the right way to go. He dreaded the invitational hymn part of the closing of the service, because he felt that every eye in the church was looking down his neck. The others had taken that step down the aisle and had made their public confession.

He was limp-kneed and uncomfortable when the Reverend asked the congregation of local farm folks to stand and sing hymn number 132. His mother handed him a hymnal open to the page. At the top he saw in bold letters the title of the song, "Jesus is Calling."

Ernie felt the urge to step out in the aisle and take those few steps forward where the Reverend Beebe stood waiting with outstretched hands. Beebe was a big man with long, strong arms.

Suddenly, one of his classmates, George Beard walked past their pew as he headed down front. Ab, as George was called, was a close buddy of Ernest's and he too had red hair. Feeling the emotional pull, Ernest thought it would be easier now to take those few steps. The minister announced in a loud voice, "And now we will sing the last verse."

His feet wouldn't move! Surely the Lord was tugging at him. He felt the power of the spirit as his mother put her hand on his frail shoulder. Before he knew it, he was standing out in the aisle looking straight at the beaming preacher, who had "Glory to God" written all over his face!

Four other young people joined that night, including Carleton Mack and one of the Kerns girls. After the service, the members and neighbors of the Bono Methodist Church lined up to congratulate and bless these new members in Christ. Aunt Mary was the first to hug and kiss him. His mother and father were proud of him. Ernest was now on the right road and was unlikely to get sidetracked with smoking, drinking, and chasing flirty girls. Life would be more serious now . . . or so they thought!

A small, black booklet, *The Probationer's Companion*, filled out and signed by Reverend Charles E. Beebe, was presented to Ernest the very next Sunday. The "Certificate of Probation" on the inside fly leaf certified that "Ernest Pyles was received on probation in the Dana Charge of the Bono Methodist Episcopal Church in the Northwest Indiana Conference on February 9, 1914."

Due to the misspelling of the name Pyle by Reverend Beebe, from this date on in school and in the neighborhood, Ernest Taylor Pyle acquired a new name: Ernest Pyles. The farm boys often needled him about the new nickname, "Pyles." They all knew what having piles meant to the older generation. Despite all of the precautions and warnings from his mother, Ernest Pyle occasionally added an "s" to his name just to show the pranksters that their humor was not really hitting the mark! His mother did not appreciate this one bit, of course.

After studying *The Probationer's Companion* in conjunction with *Pilgrim's Progress*, the new joiners of the Bono Church had to take an examination from Reverend Beebe, who started his instruction by stating, "You have entered on a new life. Suffer a few words of counsel. The way is untried. You have never passed this way before. This *Companion* may provide a guide and true friend. It at least lends you a sympathetic hand. Let us study the life you are to pursue, with suggestions of help. Let us study the church that you will soon become a member of, and let us study together."

Ernest made an honest attempt to study the handbook and learn the correct answers. Although the language was baroque and vague, and the theology and the history of the Methodist church was not as interesting as a "Smith and Street" western magazine, he passed the test. He now received a "Certificate of Membership" in his handbook, signed by The Reverend Charles E. Beebe, who warranted that Ernest Taylor "Pyles" had been baptized and properly recommended by a full member of the Bono Methodist Episcopal Church on May 3, 1914.

Because the name "Pyles" appeared on the two most important church certificates, Ernest Taylor Pyle's enthusiasm for serious religious commitment waned as soon as summer arrived. At the age of 13, Ernie placed his copy of *The Probationer's Companion* in the back corner of the chest of drawers in his room, and it stayed there, seldom used. Many other books and magazines now had precedence, as Ernest liked the excitement of horses, airplanes, automobiles, and dangerous things. He kept his walls pasted with pictures of sporting activities. He wanted to be a baseball player, but he knew he was way too small.

Although Ernest was now a bona fide member of the Bono Methodist Church, he was no more active than he had to be in the activities of the young people. Will and Maria Pyle did not push their son into the religious activities of the church. They hoped their exemplary dedication to the Christian way of life would be sufficient motivation. Ernie was smart, when he found a subject that interested him, but the endless strange names and places mentioned in the Bible usually left him staring out the window. His favorite chapters were the writings of Luke, the medical doctor and scribe, and of Paul, who underwent so much abuse and torture but could not be shaken.

Breakfast at the Pyle household came after the barnyard chores were done and the kitchen stove had caught on, warming the cold east side of the Pyle house. It was a small kitchen, but adequate. On cold winter mornings, Maria, Will, and Ernest ate their breakfast at a side table in the corner by the south window. Every breakfast, every dinner, every supper was preceded by a prayer of Thanksgiving by either Maria or Will Pyle. They were good Christian people and they worked hard to stay out of debt and keep improving their farm and their home life. All of this had a profound effect upon their son.

The Pyle family had a set schedule for every Sunday. Some of the neighbors even set their clocks by the clatter of the Pyle buggy passing by on the gravel road, on their way to the Bono Church. As they passed by the homesteads of their neighbors, all that Ernie could think was that his friends and parents were probably saying, "There go the Pyles . . . .," and Ernie thought for sure he could hear laughing trailing after them each and every Sunday morning.

By early 1916 there were over 400 cars in Vermillion County, and there were rumblings of war in Europe. The farmers prospered. Aunt Mary had raised a bumper chicken crop, despite her husband trying to keep a litter of pet skunks in the barn. Aunt Mary was hard on any of the varmints that might raid her flock, and the skunks were no exception. She raised Buff Orpingtons and lots of them. While George Bales was dreaming of raising a new strain of soybeans or yellow "Bonanza" oats, Aunt Mary was keeping up with the neighbors.

During the school months of Ernie's sophomore year in high school, the community bustled with activities for the farm children, who were trucked to school in horse-drawn hacks driven by local farmers paid by the county trustee. Although Ernest was not an "A" student, like Paul Sturm and Mariam Bales, he made some "B's" and a good splattering of "C's". After all, the Helt

Township High School, named after the prominent Helt family, was there just east of the church on the north side of the graveled road; because activities at the high school, church, and the Eastern Star Lodge, took most of the Pyle family's social time, an over-active social life may have contributed to Ernest's lack of standing as a whiz-bang student at the top of his class.

One thing is certain, however, homework or no homework, wherever Maria and Will Pyle went, Ernest was sure to go. If a neighbor was sick or poorly, or needed comforting, the Pyle family was there with a baked hen and noodles, or a sack of fresh apples, or a pan of green beans — it all depended upon the season. They were the kind of neighbors everyone wanted and it was the kind of education that is not recorded on a report card.

Ernest's high school life was the central focus of the fall and winter months, certainly; but, by March of each year, all of the students began getting restless. The sap began to stir. Yellow buds popped out on the forsythia. The ewes had their lambs. The incubator in the Pyle dining room was full of warm eggs waiting for the moment to hatch. Will Pyle worried that the inevitable cold snap would sneak up and ruin his early garden. School let out early in April because of crop-planting time, when every able-bodied male was needed on the farm — and all the while, Ernest Pyle was getting charged up for summer vacation.

However, in the spring of 1916 the Pyle family was not destined to be master tillers of the soil like Dr. John Sturm, who had all of that technical information from his alma mater, Purdue, or like Harry and George Bales, who spent long days spreading manure from the barn on the clay spots in their fields. No, the Pyle family had discovered another dimension to farming.

Several new houses and barns were under renovation. For three years in a row, the crops were good and the prices had held on poultry, livestock, and wool. Consequently, the time was good for new construction. Harry Bales had a corn crib in the making, Sammy Elder started building his brick house and large wooden barn at Tyson Corner, Claude Lockridge was adding a second bedroom to the old Bob Webster place, Dr. Sturm was building a new home in front of the old house which was left standing, and the Kuhns were underway with their new two-story farm house. (They needed more bedrooms because their family increased by one each year!)

With opportunity all about him, Will Pyle sharpened up his saws, put new handles on his claw and shingle hammers, dusted off his miter box, bought a new bubble-level gauge, picked up two new carpenter aprons at Rice and Scott Hardware, and went to work at the Kuhns' house as a carpenter. He was a first-rate cabinet man and had good imagination in design and construction. During the spring, he worked only part time on the Kuhns' new house, which was just across the fence from the Pyle barn, but Will knew that in the fall, when the corn was cultivated and laid by, and the grain threshed, he would be able to devote more time to his first love — carpentry.

Dr. Sturm called Will Pyle on the telephone one evening in late May 1916. "Will, I've about decided to drive over to Indianapolis and see the races, but I need to leave a day early due to the heavy traffic on route 36. I know Ernest likes cars, so I thought maybe he could come along with Paul and Bill Bales and me. It would be a great chance for him to see the Indy 500."

"That's sure nice of you, Doc," replied Will Pyle, "maybe I could substitute for Ernest on the spur line for that one day." Ernie had landed a job with the railroad working a slip shovel, building a grade for the spur line running south to the Bono coal mine. "Don't want him to miss a day. He might lose his job."

Just after the turn of the century, as many as 50 makes of cars were being produced in Indiana's capital city, including the world-famous Dusenberg. There soon was a great need for a reliable and adequate testing ground for all the new cars and innovations that were being introduced into the market. Eventually, a group of five friends opened an Indianapolis racetrack in 1910. The first roadbed, a disastrous combination of tar and crushed rock, was not successful, so the next year the entire track was laid with brick paving, a job that took, remarkably, only 63 days to complete! Naturally, someone decided to call it "The Brickyard", a nickname that stuck. It was a big news story and people from all over the Midwest came to see the "500", so named because the race required 200 laps around the brickyard to reach the final tape. Newspapers carried the event every year on the front page. Ernie Pyle, like every other farm boy at the time, believed speeding racecars spelled romance, fame, and guts. He dreamed of the whine of a 12-cylinder job, the biting wind in his face, the pinch of his goggles, the smell of burned-out oil and the roar of the crowd — this could be his Indy 500. Ernie secretly hoped that he could get his Ford coupe up to 40 mph some day; but to think of a racer going 100 mph, it was just too amazing, to say the least.

The second year of the race, in May of 1911, had a field of some 40 cars. That race took almost seven hours to complete. And the total of $25,000 was distributed among the top 12 winners. By 1916, the crowds had grown ten-fold. People continued to flock to Indianapolis by the thousands.

Doc Sturm had his Overland greased and oiled for the long trip. He took off the side curtains and added a spare tire on the back above the bumper. Doc, Paul, Ernest, and Bill took off at 5:00 a.m. on Saturday. It was just turning daylight. They headed east down the graveled road by Oll Staats apple orchard.

They then went down into the holler, where they crossed the red covered bridge. When they finally intersected with Highway 36, the main road to Indianapolis, there was already a solid procession of cars.

For miles ahead they could see great columns of road dust billowing into the morning sky. On across the Wabash River Bridge at Montezuma, on east past the brick plant, over the Little Leatherwood, through Rockville, the county seat of Park County, over Big Raccoon Creek — all seen through a cloud of dust. They passed many cars pulled off to the side of the road, where disgruntled passengers were fixing flat tires or searching for radiator water. The road was gravel all the way into the outskirts of Indianapolis. Doc figured they could average 20 mph considering the stops along the way.

Maria had fixed some sandwiches and Carrie Sturm had baked a big chocolate cake for the boys. Just past Danville, Doc pulled off on a side road so the boys could stretch and eat some food, which tasted a little like dust since everyone and the countryside were covered with road dust. The thermos of cold water was much in demand.

Doc wanted to get into the city early so he could find a motel for the night and then a parking place close to the speedway since the whole area would become a solid sea of people and Model T Fords by race time.

Race time! It was a deafening roar of power Ernie would never forget. The smell of hot castor oil hung like a curtain over the spectators. Round and round went the racers, with Ernest watching every minute. In his mind he was already planning how he could become a race driver.

After the winner had been declared and the huge crowds had melted away from the track, Doc got his little group of farm boys back in the Overland and headed west to Vermillion County through the same persistent cloud of dust that seemed to rise to the very heavens. It was an exciting adventure. Ernest Taylor Pyle had experienced free passage to and from Indianapolis, the home of the most-attended one-day sporting event in America!

It was far after midnight when Doc Sturm delivered a sleepy boy to the Pyle residence. Ernie was sure he would never forget the experience. To be a speed king was now, for certain, his prime ambition in life. He swore to himself, that at every possible occasion, he would pick up the broadcast of the "500" on the radio. In his dreams he could still hear the whine of those high-powered racing cars and the smell of the burning oil and rubber.

While Will was doing the carpenter's chores, Maria Pyle was alone measuring the rooms for wallpaper. It was only natural that Ernest would end up as the helper-handyman for the Will-and-Maria building team. No one worked for less and no one could do a better job. Maria, always sensing opportunity, encouraged Will to rent out the farming so they could devote much of their time to the more lucrative occupation of building. Maria had a good mind for business; after all, she had created a very profitable chicken ranch at the Mound long before it was even an acceptable practice in Indiana. She incubated more eggs, set more hens, raised more fryers, and sold more "hen fruit" than any of her neighbors. This was their bread and butter money, guaranteed each year.

In the meantime, Ernest learned how to follow a chalk line with the ripsaw, and how to cut a square beam with the cross-cut saw. His father taught him how to lath the walls in a newly studded room, and how to hang a wooden door. His mother ordered a new pasting table for their wallpapering project from

Sears Roebuck. It was a folding table on which the wallpaper could be trimmed and pasted. Ernest worked closely with his mother to learn just how much paste to slap on the backside of the wallpaper, which had been cut in exact lengths by his father. Working from two separate stepladders, Maria and Will, with Ernest as helper, could hang a room of wallpaper before noontime.

Next came Ernie's apprenticeship on how to paint the interior and exterior of houses, barns, corncribs, hen houses, tool sheds, wood sheds, and porches. The Pyle family would tackle any job, no matter how difficult or how far away it might be. Ernest learned the art of painting, glazing windows, and trimming sash.

Ernie learned the art of painting with white lead and oil. The Pyle family always was in demand as there was an acute shortage of construction and tradesmen during the summer months because every able-bodied man was needed in the fields. By the end of summer 1916, Ernest had saved enough money to buy his own clothes for school. His mother and father took him to Dana to visit Rhoades and Sons Dry Goods Store, where he was promptly fitted out with new blue work shirts, a pair of wool pants, a pair of new overalls, a cap with earflaps folded inside, some cotton socks, and a pair of shoes that laced up in front and a brown wool sweater.

For his 16th birthday, Ernest Taylor Pyle received the surprise of his life. He had worked hard all summer with his parents and they continued to prosper. His present was a brand new Model-T Ford runabout, which cost his father the tidy sum of $328.00. It was shiny black, with two big headlights for night driving. Ernest promptly had the word "Shag," the nickname given to him by his step-cousin, Bill Bales, painted on both doors. He quickly learned to adjust the spark and throttle levers, which were under the steering wheel. The wooden floorboard had three pedals: the clutch, the reverse, and the brake. Bill Bales installed a wire choke that came out front by the radiator so that Ernie could crank his Ford and choke it at the same time.

Up and down the dusty roads of Helt Township went Ernest Pyle, a real threat to the neighbors' poultry, which often strayed along the roadway. Once he experienced the feel of power, he would never be the same! Racecars, speedboats, and airplanes were next. It was his senior year in high school, and he dreamed a lot. He was a restless spirit, yet his mother was stern and made him toe the line.

Just after the first week back at Helt Township High School, his junior year, fall 1916, Ernest, Thad Hooker, and two other neighbor boys, all with the permission of their mothers, headed towards the big town of Clinton, Indiana, population 4,000. There was a new roller skating rink in Clinton, just 14 miles south of the Mound. They started out driving Ernie's new Model T late on Saturday afternoon, heading south through the back roads of the countryside. Just as it was getting dark and they were entering the outskirts of Clinton, their headlights went out due to a short in the electrical system.

Later that next week, after all the excitement the adventure to Clinton had generated among his friends at Bono High and when he really should have been doing his homework, Ernie wrote an account in Robert Service style of their brush with the law.

A Woeful Tale

We were on our way to Clinton on the skating rink to glide;
Max and Hank were on the door, while Jones was by my side.
We had a short! Oh! very short, and our lights were very dim.
So out jumped Hook, a match he took and lit the coal-oil glim.

We piled back in old Henry, and our hearts were full of glee;

With joyous sound we drove along although we could not see.
We turned the corner at Fairview and began to beat it south.
When all in a flash - a terrible crash, we hit Dobbin in the mouth.

The buggy was turned over, the Ford was pushed to the side.
Max and Hook were shouting, O! Look!, while Jonesy was trying to hide.
O, such commotion—I had a foolish notion of skipping out for Terre Haute,
When up jumped a man and hollered, and began to pull off his coat.

A policeman came and asked me my name — I told him Hocus P. Docus;
He grabbed my neck and kicked me, by heck! and said he was going to soak us.
So with four men in prison and 3 women dead, I will end this sorrowful tale,
Now if you're out after night, don't run with light and maybe you'll keep out of jail!

Written by the renowned villain Ernestinius Taylorium Pylo,
when he should have been studying his history.

The accident was the result of uncontrollable events, and since no one was injured, Maria and Will Pyle did not punish their son. In fact, the affair was seldom discussed and Will Pyle had the Model-T repaired and painted just like new.

***

It was the third weekend after school had started when Will Pyle, with his son, Ernest, left the house and headed west in their buggy to call on Harry Bales. It was cider-making time. The Jonathan and the Winesaps trees throughout the country were sagging with plump red apples. Many had started falling to the ground, and experience had taught Ernie and the rest of the boys that those were usually the wormy ones.

Behind Harry's barn was a two-acre apple orchard, nestled comfortably inside a white oak, split-rail fence. Harry's grandfather, Captain Caleb, had planted this quaint little orchard shortly after his return from the Civil War. "If anything ever happens to Clarence, I want his wife to have plenty of apples for all of those kids," he used to tell his neighbors. Clarence Campbell had served in the Civil War and limped badly from a leg wound he received during a skirmish near Lexington. Captain Caleb felt a strong sense of responsibility to the Campbell family, which was trying to eke out a living on the 7 acres just east of the woods.

Now the orchard was deep in blue grass, with the gnarled old apple trees sagging with dark red blushing apples. When there was a good crop, there was cider making in the back of the Bales' barn. It was a warm autumn day and Harry had the cider press all washed down and positioned inside the barn in the back walkway.

"Will, you and the boys take those gunny sacks and bushel baskets and fill as many as you can," suggested Harry who was lining up a collection of large jars and several jugs. "Have the boys shake off those low branches, as they're the best apples."

After filling 10 gunny sacks and seven bushel baskets with fresh picked apples, Will Pyle and the three boys started carrying the apples along the fence row to the backside of the barn where Harry awaited them. It was only ten rods from the barn to the orchard, so it did not take long to drag all the sacks and baskets into the cider press.

With eager eyes, the boys watched Harry and Will pour the first bushel into the round slotted hopper, then swing the round wooden lid in place and attach the cranking wheel. Round and round it spun until the apples popped and squirted forth with fresh apple juice.

"Here, Ernie, keep that bucket under the spout as it won't take long to fill it full," chuckled Harry who took great joy in working with the boys. "This is real, for-sure apple cider you're looking at, Paul," said Harry noticing that the boys had picked up the delicious aroma of fresh apple cider.

Will and Harry kept turning the wheel as the apple juice ran like water down the wooden spigot splattering so gently into the large bucket. The foam oozed up through the golden liquid and the aroma of fresh apples permeated the walkway of the barn.

"Here's what we're going to do. Now for each sack or basket you helped carry in here, you get one cup full of fresh cider to drink, right out of the bucket," Harry remarked rather casually, taking a large blue-and-white enameled cup from a paper sack behind him.

"I helped on three baskets," replied Ernest.

"I helped on four," said Carl. He always helped his Uncle Harry with the barnyard chores.

"Paul, you brought in four didn't you?" asked Will Pyle, winking at Harry as they kept the wheel turning on the cider press.

"Well, get started drinking, boys. This is the best cider you'll ever taste, and it will put hair on your chest," said Harry, spurring them on.

What followed was a barnyard event that would become legend throughout the neighborhood. Although the cider was delicious, what the boys did not know was that fresh cider in an excess amount acted as a severe laxative. While the boys were busy discussing how much work they had done and drinking cup after cup of fresh and delightful apple cider, Harry Bales and Will Pyle patiently kept turning the wheel on the press, pouring in more apples and waiting for the lightning to strike. The afternoon wore on.

Suddenly, like a body slung from a medieval catapult, Paul Sturm vaulted the barn door and disappeared from sight. He didn't get far, however, before he had his britches down. In two shakes of a lamb's tail, Ernie had joined him in the hog lot, where they were now partially concealed by some tall jimson weeds. Corncobs were plentiful, formality and privacy absent.

Laughing till their ribs hurt, Harry Bales had to support himself on the barn door, while Will Pyle, catching his breath, was barely able to call to the boys, "Hurry up and get in here." They both laughed some more. "Harry and I can't finish up until you can help us."

A new round of laughter erupted when young Ernest wailed from the boys' retreat, "I can't get my overalls pulled up till I have to go again." The men laughed so hard they cried. And it was a story that would most likely bring laughs for many years to come.

The work crew was able to get back to work, however, after a short while, far wiser if not happier for the experience. The last of the apples were processed and the juice was safely stored in five-gallon jars. Harry and Will loaded a five-gallon jar in the Pyle buggy. Harry gave Will a quart fruit jar filled with the murky brown liquid.

"Here's the 'mother' for your cider, Will."

On the way home, Ernest asked his father, "What is this funny stuff in the jar, Papa?"

"That's what they call the 'mother' or 'starter'. You mix it in the apple juice so it will ferment and turn the cider to vinegar."

As Maria and Will carefully stored the big jar of apple juice on the back porch and covered it over with cheesecloth to keep out the flies, Ernest headed for the backyard. From that day on, Ernest was not overly fond of cider, although he did learn the necessary art of making homemade vinegar.

⋅◇⟫◐⟪◇⋅

It was the spring of 1917. Because of his small size and shyness, Ernie just wasn't the high-school-Romeo type. In fact, he did not participate in any of the high school sports because of his frail build. From childhood, Ernie was susceptible to colds, croup, sore throats, allergies, runny noses and chiggers. If a mosquito or sweat bee was within a mile of Ernie, he ended up getting "bit."

The Helt Township High School at Bono was only three miles south of the high school at Dana. One reason Dana High School had more that twice as many students was that it had a very active athletic program, while Bono had only a baseball team. Although Ernie worked hard in the summers with his dad, doing fieldwork, barnyard chores, and handyman tasks, he still didn't develop into the big, rugged, farm-boy type as had his cousins Lincoln and Sam Saxton, or his next-door neighbors, Paul Sturm and Carl Crane, who, of course, because they were such good athletes, decided to attend high school at Dana.

Most boys raised in a small country town have some pretty colorful experiences with athletics and girls. Ernie kind of struck out in both departments. His first real sweetheart was Florence Kuhns. One Sunday afternoon, when her mother and father came by to visit the Frank Kuhns, the Pyle's next-door neighbors, Ernest encountered his first taste of romance purely by accident.

There never was a time in Ernie's boyhood when he was considered to be the next farmer in line for the Pyle farm. He just wasn't the farmer-type, although he loved the out-of-doors, horses and dogs and the touch of the soil. It was his home country and he grew up right there on the Mound with a gob of cow manure under each heel. But he had something else, and his mother knew it. Ernest's mother had watched over him carefully for 16 years, and she knew there was something special about Ernie. It was her responsibility to see that he got every chance in the world to "amount to something."

"Mama, I would like to go over to the Kuhns this afternoon and play. Can I?"

"You mean 'May I?'"

"Yes, Mama."

"You change your clothes as I don't want you to tear a hole in those Sunday britches."

"All right, Mama. We're going to play baseball down by the schoolhouse."

"You be careful and don't get hurt."

"I'll be careful, Mama."

"Tell Mary Alice I have her dress almost finished, and if she wants to, come over and I'll fit it."

"I'll tell her. I'm going to take Shep with me!" The back door slammed shut as Ernest yelled " Goodbye," making a flying departure for the Kuhns' farm.

The new Kuhns' house had just been completed. There were a lot of finishing touches that Will and Maria had made to the house. The front porch looked south over the rolling pasture where the small, boarded-up Mound Schoolhouse rested in silence under two large elm trees. A narrow gravel road came up the hill to the house, which was already bulging with Frank and Lelia Kuhns and their 10 active children. Living next door to the Kuhns family provided Ernest much joy and activity. There was always someone to play with next door, and the stile behind the Pyle barn accommodated lots of bare feet.

Later that evening, Ernest came trudging home about sundown. As he came by the Pyle barn, he stopped to talk with his mother and father who were just finishing the evening milking and turning the cows out to graze.

Standing in the barn door, Ernest grinned at his father, who had a full bucket of milk in each hand.

"Did you have a good time, Ernest?" asked his father.

"Yes, Papa, but I'm sure tired from playing baseball."

"Who won?"

"We didn't keep score."

Maria Pyle unstrapped the halter on the last cow and pushed her toward the open door. "Did you see Mary Alice?" asked his mother.

"Oh, yes. She's real happy that you're making that dress, Mama. She had her cousin visiting her, Mama." After a few moments, Ernie softly asked, "Who is Florence Kuhns?"

"That's Mont Kuhns' daughter, isn't it, Will?" Maria looked at Ernie with mounting interest.

"I believe so. They moved into St. Bernice and he's an engineer on one of those big locomotives"

"Ernest, I believe Frank and O.M. Kuhns are first cousins, so Mary Alice and Florence would be second cousins." Maria smiled. "Why are you so interested in Florence?"

"She's real pretty, Mama, and I like her brother Cassel."

"How old is Florence?"

"She's a year or two younger than me, I reckon," said Ernie as he left the barn.

In a few moments, Maria mused, "Will, I think we've got a lovesick boy on our hands." She smiled a mother's bitter-sweet smile as she put the chain over the post of the gate and started back to the house with her husband.

"I reckon so," grinned Will Pyle under his neatly cropped mustache. "The Kuhns are good people."

So started the first romantic venture for Ernest Taylor Pyle. It was a new experience for him. Florence Kuhns was to become an important girlfriend as the months and years went by. The Pyle and the Kuhns families would remain the closest of friends.

It was spring of 1918 and Bono was now an important coal-mining town. Just west of town a mile or so was one of the richest veins of soft coal ever discovered in the state. Because there was no high school in St. Bernice, the newcomers Mont and Bertha Kuhns had to send their four children, including Florence, Ernie's new flame, to Helt Township High School, which was a good six miles away. With 10 cousins from the Frank Kuhns' family in school there, the four new Kuhns kids fit right in at Bono High. Ernie was instantly smitten with Florence, who was a year behind him. Her brother, Cassell, was a junior, and he and Ernie became the closest of friends.

On April 2, 1917, came the thunderbolt — war was declared against Germany! People all over the country immediately readjusted their values. Able-bodied men in Helt Township dropped their plows and signed up. The fever to join up was rampant in the community, but Will and Maria Pyle told Ernest he would finish high school and that was that. His Aunt Mary would give him no sympathy either. Education came first. He could always go to war, if that was what he wanted to do. Doc Sturm had told Will Pyle that he wanted Paul to finish High School before he would let him go into the military reserve.

Thad Hooker, Ernie's closest friend, hurriedly joined the army and was shipped to Texas for rifle training. Several others in his high school heeded the call-to-arms. They became the real heroes, in Ernest's eyes. And he wanted dearly to join their ranks.

Throughout Ernie's senior year, 1916 to 1917, there was

lots of talk about the big war and the terrible "Huns" who had started it all. Grisly pictures of the doughboys in the trenches began to appear in the newspapers. There were photos of "Big Bertha", the German's huge cannon, of dead horses, rats, mud, barbed wire, and sad pictures of our dead boys. There were colorful stories of gallant men in fantastic flying machines, getting into dogfights high in the noonday sun. Through it all, Ernest tried to study his geometry and history. Had it not been for that cute little girl named Florence Kuhns, who was now a junior at Helt Township High School, he might have just quit and run off to war.

His mother sensed the restless spirit in her son and kept reassuring him that without the high school diploma, he would end up as a potato peeler.

Vernon Blythe, a fine young man from Dana, was reported missing in action on the Western front. Mr. and Mrs. Roy Thompson received a telegram that their son, Harry, had died just before he was to be shipped overseas. Shortly thereafter, Bernard Nickels was killed in action in the Argonne. This brought the war to everyone's living room. People were shocked at the casualties. Ernest was now even more determined to do his share.

Would graduation ever come? Several of the boys at the Bono School left to join up in the military. When Thad left, Ernest was heartbroken as well as envious. Thad was going to Texas, where they would make a man out of him. He was a frail lad like Ernest.

Graduation day finally arrived on Friday, May 3, 1918. It had been a long, wet springtime, and the sun finally skidded through the clouds that afternoon in Bono. Friends and relatives of the new graduates were there early in order to get the best seats in the auditorium.

After the pledge of allegiance, led by Mr. Ralph Shields, the superintendent, Miss Mary Kitzsmiller, the Latin and English teacher, read off the list of the graduating class of 1918. The class had chosen as their motto, "Climb, though the rocks be rugged." A row of eight empty chairs was on the stage facing the audience. The chair on the end was draped with the American flag. Everyone knew that would have been Thad's chair.

"Marie McDowell, Carrie M. Malone, Mariam J. Bales, Mabel A. Rideout, Marzelle Kerns, Aikman Foncannon, Ernest T. Pyle, and Thad K. Hooker in absentia," reported Miss Kitzsmiller in her official capacity.

"Now will the graduating class of 1918 please be seated?" she responded after the procession of seven had reached their respective chairs. It would be a long and miserable afternoon for Ernest, one he would remember for a long time and one that would shape and define his future.

When Ernest saw the draped flag on Thad's chair, which he was seated next to, a large lump had welled up in his throat. He did not hear the stimulating and inspiring talk Reverend O. C. Chivington gave. His mind was far, far away from Bono. All he could think was that Thad had been killed and his country needed him. "U.S. Navy, here I come," he kept telling himself. He would be a sailor in uniform and, who knows, the girls may like him even better. After all, there must be some special appeal to that Navy uniform!

His mother and father were seated right next to Aunt Mary and Uncle George in the front row. Directly behind them was the Kuhns family and Mr. and Mrs. Harry Bales. Florence smiled at him when his name was called to come forth and receive the much-cherished diploma. He saw her and she watched him. He'd have a sweetheart at home if he joined the Navy. Someone to write to. And when the war was over, he would have someone to come home to. Someone waiting at the railroad station just like the pictures in the newspapers showed it.

But in a despicable twist of fate, once again Ernest Taylor Pyle went down in humiliation before his peers. For the first time that day, he looked at the graduation program. His was the only misspelled name in his class! Somehow, someway an "s" had been added to the name of Pyle. Once again, Ernie was reminded of the cruel and mocking laughs he often imagined his classmates having behind his back. His parents and good friends never mentioned it again, of course, but Ernie couldn't help thinking on this final day before he would become a man, "One day they're going to spell my name right. I swear, one day, they'll know for sure that my name is Ernest Taylor Pyle."

After the congratulations, the cake and coffee, the handshakes and hugs, the biggest day of his life was coming to an end. Florence looked prettier than ever to him.

"When are you leaving, Ernest?" she inquired in a soft voice.

"Just as soon as I get my orders, Florence," he replied rather bashfully. Ernie was going to miss Florence greatly, but just as he had learned to block out his humiliation for the joke on his name, he put a good face on the sadness of having to leave home and the one girl he loved.

Despite his mother's last minute pleas and sad eyes, Ernie Pyle was on his way to Peoria, Illinois, to enroll in the Naval Reserve. Upon signing up he was immediately sent to Champaign, where he went through boot camp and lived in a converted gymnasium with some 200 other eager-to-be seamen. He dreamed of riding the high seas, battling the big waves and seeing foreign ports. All summer he trained in boot camp. He was a neat and meticulous sailor, and when he wore his Navy uniform, he actually looked larger than 125 pounds.

He had a lot of time to write letters, and he did so at every occasion to avoid the boredom of "combat duty" in the Illinois cornfields. He missed Thad, he missed Florence, and he missed his mama, but he was determined to see the world. He was going to make sure that when he returned to Dana and to Helt Township High School everyone would know his name.

"Come Hell or high water," Ernie said aloud, "they're going to know my name."

Chapter 10

A One Man Army

Two old friends sat on a curb in the quiet little town of Dana, Indiana. It was an unusually pleasant day in September of 1944. One of these men was Ernie Pyle, who had just returned, exhausted, from a three-year stint covering World War II in Europe for Scripps Howard. His daily columns from the infantry trenches had been appearing in daily newspapers all over the country. The Allies had liberated Paris in August and the Germans were now in retreat. Ernie was home for some well-deserved rest and recuperation. The other fellow, who was just about Ernie's age, was George Potter, one of his oldest and closest friends. George and Ernie had known each other since second grade; they had a lot of catching up to do.

"Ernie, remember those rowdy trips on that little school hack when we were going to Bono?"

"Sure do. It was either you or your brother Oll who got me to chewing tobacco, remember that George?"

"Yep, we used to hang out the back door of that hack and spit at rocks," chuckled George.

The Potter boys were the hardest workers that Ernie had ever met. For as long as Ernie could remember, their motto had been simple and straightforward: Work hard and you'll get there. They may have started out with nothing but the clothes on their backs, but they were the most respected, hard-working boys in the community. Ernie was not surprised in the least that they had turned their poor background into great success.

"You brothers are an inspiration to the whole community, George. You must own about half of the county now, don't you?"

George chuckled, "Not quite half, Ernie."

When they were young, George, Oll, and Charlie Potter had made a vow among themselves that someday they would accumulate enough money to buy out the men who had taken advantage of their dad. These men were landowners, so it would take a heap of money and time. Over the years, the Potter brothers had built their small trucking business into a sizeable company, and only then had they branched out into land, cattle, and grain elevators.

"Papa says you boys bought out many of the farms."

"Yep. Do you remember when we were kids, when I promised that my brothers and me were going to buy out every man that had looked down on our dad?"

Ernie nodded his head, "I do remember Mama talking about some shameful men who hired your dad for 50 cents a day to dig ditches, clear fences, and do the hardest work on the farm."

"Well, there were five on our list, and now we own all of the land of four of them," said George. "Not bad for country hicks, is it Ernie?"

George and Ernie sat in silence for a few minutes, looking down Main Street. Finally, George said, "Dad was quite a father,

Ernie. I don't know how he did it, but he raised us up to be pretty good boys." George was a big fellow, but Ernie could see he was deeply affected by the memory of his dad.

"What is Charlie doing now, George?" asked Ernie. Charlie was the real brain behind the family's financial success, but Ernie truly admired him for the way he always cared about the little guy. He was always giving time and money to the poor and destitute in the county.

"He's in charge of all of the farms, Ernie," said George. "That column you wrote about us kind of put us on the map. Our cattle-hauling trucks have been very successful and our farms are doing great." George leaned over and spit a string of tobacco juice halfway across the red-bricked Main Street.

"Papa said that Oll was getting married to a real pretty girl up here in Dana," said Ernie. "He said he's now the sheriff of Vermillion County."

"You know Oll, he's just an easy-going big guy who can work rings around the guy next to him," said George.

Ernie looked across the street at the storefronts along Main Street. "Dana seems to have shrunk from the way I remembered it, George. But it sure is nice to have a place to come back to for a while before I have to hit the road again."

George said, "Ernie, why don't you just hang it up. The war in Europe is just about over; you don't need to stretch your luck."

"No, George, I've got to leave tomorrow. They're sending me out to the Pacific to cover the Marines. Jack Bales is stationed on Saipan, flying with a B-29 group and I want to see him. I also understand that Bobby is over in England flying a B-24. It's truly remarkable how those Bales boys took off from Dana when the War started . . . . George, I've got this feeling I might not be coming back, so I want you to watch out for Papa and Aunt Mary, okay?"

"I will Ernie, but I want you to get back here safe and sound. And by the time you do, me and my brothers just might have picked up that 5th farm, for sure," smiled George Potter. "By the way," he continued, "do you remember when my dog was shot, Ernie?"

"Sure do," said Ernie. "Why do you ask?"

"Well, my dad told me afterwards that the world always gives back to us what we give out to others. I've made my peace with the mean-spirited and negative people of this world, Ernie. I happen to believe that forgiving others and doing good creates its own reward. Ernie, you've done this country a world of good. Keep on telling it like it is, and we'll see each other in the hereafter if not before."

Ernie looked at George, thinking all the while how happy he was that his life as a journalist had introduced him to so many good men of integrity. America would always be strong, he thought, provided that decent and honorable men like George Potter kept working the front lines of industry and commerce, and, although he hoped it would never come again, war.

"So long, George," said Ernie as they shook hands. "I hope one day someone decides to build a monument to you and your brothers to remind kids everywhere that anything is possible with hard work, honesty, and determination."

From Supreme Headquarters, Allied Expeditionary Force, Dwight D. Eisenhower,
to Ernie Pyle, December 15, 1944

Dear Ernie:

A few days ago I wrote you a note acknowledging receipt of your latest book [Brave Men]. Now I have read it.

I enjoyed it all. The last chapter strikes me ¾ although I am a bit hesitant to admit it because of a most flattering personal reference ¾ as a remarkably fine piece of writing. I think it well expresses the reactions of decent people to this bloody business.

But the one thing in your book that hits me most forcibly is a short sentence at the top of the fifth page where you announce yourself as a rabid, one-man army, going full out to tell the truth about the infantry combat soldier. This sentence gives me an idea for a useful postwar job. I should like you to authorize a hundred per cent increase in your army, (I mean in size, not in quality) and let me join. I will furnish the "brass" and you, as in all other armies, would do the work. In addition, I will promise a lot of enthusiasm because I get so eternally tired of the general lack of understanding of what the infantry soldier endures that I have come to the conclusion that education along this one simple line might do a lot toward promoting future reluctance to engage in war. The difference between you and me in regard to this infantry problem is that you can express yourself eloquently upon it; I get so fighting mad because of the general lack of appreciation of real heroism ¾ which is the uncomplaining acceptance of unendurable conditions ¾ that I become completely inarticulate. Anyway, I volunteer. If you want me you don't have to resort to the draft.

Thanks again for your book.

With best wishes,
Sincerely, Dwight D. Eisenhower

Feb. 27, 1945

Dear General Ike

Your grand letter of Dec. 15 has just now showed up. It was a long time reaching me. It doesn't require an answer, but I wanted to tell you how much I appreciate it anyway.

Yes, I think I'll allow you to join my army. But I think we're both fighting a losing cause — for I've found that no matter how much we talk, or write, or show pictures, people who have not actually been in war are incapable of having any real conception of it. I don't really blame the people. Some of them try hard to understand. But the world of the infantryman is a world so far removed from anything normal that it can be no more than academic to the average person.

As you know, I've spent two-and-a-half years carrying the torch for the foot-soldier, and I think I have helped make America conscious of and sympathetic toward him, but I haven't' made them feel what he goes through. I believe it's impossible. But I'll keep on trying.

I'm out in the Pacific now. Came about six weeks ago. It's very hard for me to get adjusted to the tempo of things out here. Distances are so vast; the time lag between planning and execution is so great; living conditions are so much better; most of the time you're just preparing for or traveling to a war. Now and then I have to pinch myself to realize this is war.

As much as I grew to hate the war, I miss my friends and the camaraderie of misery of the Western Front. But lots of the boys both in the Mediterranean and on the German front continue to write me and give me all the little front-line gossip, so I don't feel entirely lost. I suppose I shall be out here in the Pacific for a year or more. Are you all coming over to join us when you get your business finished?

I had to chuckle when I read your letter, and others you've written me. For some evil soul started a rumor in Washington, shortly after I came home from France last fall, that you had kicked me out of the European Theater for something I wrote that displeased you. The Rumormonger would have enjoyed reading over my shoulder. I wonder why there have to be people in the world like that?

Please give my best to Butch and Tex and General "Beetle." And to General Bradley again when you see him. I had the pleasure of squiring his wife and daughter around Washington some last November. And good wishes to you. I don't know how you have stood up under the burdens you've had to bear these past three years. I fervently hope the bloody mess is soon finished.

Most sincerely,
Ernie Pyle

On April 18, 1945, Ernie Pyle was killed in a jeep a few hundred yards outside the village of Ie Shima. At the site of Ernie's death, those he served with put up a simple marker—

At This Spot
The 77th Infantry Division
Lost a Buddy
Ernie Pyle
18 April 1945

President Roosevelt had passed away only a few days before the news of Ernie Pyle's death reached Washington.

President Truman, interrupted during a news conference, said, "The nation is quickly saddened again by the death of Ernie Pyle. No man in this war has so well told the story of the American fighting man as American fighting men wanted it told. He deserves the gratitude of all his countrymen."

And when General Eisenhower heard of Ernie Pyle's death, he said, "The GIs in Europe — and that means all of us here — have lost one of our best and most understanding friends."

This grainy photograph was taken by George Potter shortly after the Elder house had been moved up to Main Street in Dana, Indiana. This is the little tenant house where Ernie Pyle was born on August 3, 1900. It mysteriously burned to the ground in 1968, after having been vacant for several years. A primitive three-bedroom house, it was built about 1870 for hired hands and their families who worked the Elder farm. Ernie's parents moved into the tenant house in November 1989 and lived there for eleven months, moving back to the "Mound" when Ernest Taylor Pyle was two months old.

Lambert Taylor was the father of Maria, Mary, and John Taylor. He bought his 77-acre farm in 1872. Ernie always referred to the Taylor farm at the Mound as his real home. He had moved there with his parents when he was barely two months old. Over the years, Will and Maria Pyle developed their farm into a pleasant home site by steadily, consistently clearing the land for farming.

Mary and Maria Taylor had their photographs taken in Tuscola, Illinois, at the turn of the century. Maria married William Pyle when she was almost 30, and Mary married George Bales at the age of 45. Maria produced one son, Ernest Taylor Pyle, and Mary raised a stepson, William Franklin Bales. As sisters, they were inseparable.

Note the fancy attire of the Pyles and their neighbors in 1900. In the center of the back row stand Will and Maria Pyle. Mary Elizabeth, who would later married George Bales, is on the right end of the second row.

This is the home of Will and Maria Pyle, where Ernest Taylor Pyle was raised. Two months after being born in the tenant house on the Elder farm, Ernie with his parents moved back to Maria's father's farm at the "Mound." The original 3-room house was built in 1896 and was moved to its present location in 1901. Since that date, numerous addition have been made to the house by Will Pyle and his brother Quince. Both were good carpenters. Ernie's room was on the northwest corner. The front porch was the last addition to the house, which toady is owned and protected by Ed Goforth's family. The Goforths and the Pyle families were lifelong friends, both having lived in Sam Elder's tenant house as his hired hands.

The William F. Bales family settled just a mile west of the "Mound."
William Bales built his house in 1869 on 65 acres of rich farm land.
He became the highway commissioner for Vermillion County, Indiana, and
was instrumental in building many graveled roads and numerous covered
bridges.

His five children all married and settled close by in Helt Township. His
oldest daughter married Ol J. Staats, who developed the Staats Apple
Orchards a mile east of the "Mound." Frank brought the farm adjoining the
east side of his father's, while Carrie married Dr. John D. Sturm, a Purdue
veterinarian who lived directly across the road from Ernie's home place, Julie
married John Tolle, who became a prosperous farmer, and widowed George
Bales, who was a horticulturist, married Ernie's Aunt Mary.

Ernest Taylor Pyle was the pride and joy of his parents, Will and Maria Pyle. Getting this photo taken at the age of 2 was a major effort.

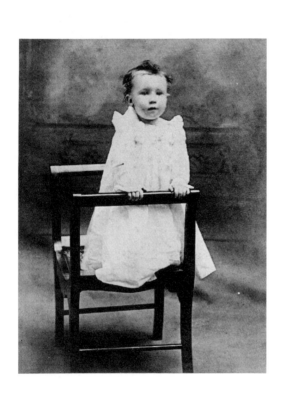

This hobby horse was ordered from Chicago through the Montgomery Ward catalogue. At the age of 4, Ernie showed definite signs of becoming a proud horseman, riding properly on his hobby horse, which is still in the family. The Pyles would give handmade gifts each Christmas and on many birthdays, using household materials such as ribbon, spools, and crepe.

The new county school at Bono was a brick compound. It provided a new venue for education in this rural country. Sadie Campbell, in the middle of the front row, was a much-loved teacher and remained in contact with Ernie all his life. Ernie stands on the very right end of the second row. The following is a list of the class, as they stand left to right.

Front Row	Second Row	Back Row
Helen Beard	Carrie Stewart	Unknown
Unknown	Mamie McDowel	Gladys Porter
Gladys Chambers	Mariam Bales Goforth	Opal Bowen
Kathleen Sweeny	Edith Pearman	Unknown
Sadie Campbell	Marie McDowel	Keene Sturm
Harvey Kerns	George Beard	Unknown
Aikman Foncannon	Unknown	Clyde Cheeswright
Unknown	Unknown	Unknown
Thad Hooker	Unknown	Herman Howard
	Dewey Newton	Unknown
	Ernest Pyle	Unknown
		Carl Crane

Ernie with Cricket as the waterboy, age 12.

Ernie Pyle at the age of 16. As a sophomore at Bono High School, he was a dashing and bashful young farm boy who liked nice clothes.

Will & Maria Pyle beside their first Ford coupe.

Maria and Will Pyle, Ernie's parents, as they appeared at his commencement exercises at Bono High School in 1918.

Notice the spelling of Ernie's last name in his commencement program.
It was an episode that had a tremendous effect on the young man.

Class Motto:

Climb, though the
Rocks be Rugged

Class Colors:
Purple and Gold.

Class Flower:
Sweet Peas.

Class Roll:
Marie McDowell
Carrie M. Malone
Mariam J. Bales
Mabel A. Rideout
Marzelle Kerns
Aikman Foncannon
Ernest T. Pyles
Thad K. Hooker

Mary E. Kitsmiller, Principal.
Ralph C. Shields, Superintendent

A graduation photo of Ernie upon finishing his senior year at Bono High School in 1918. Several of his classmates were already serving in World War I, so he promptly joined the U.S. Navy and went into the Reserve Naval Training Program in Champaign, Illinois, about 70 miles northwest of Dana. Shortly thereafter, the war ended and Ernie would head to Indiana University.

Throughout his life, Ernie shunned publicity and hated photographs, but he did have this photo taken while at Indiana University in the fall of 1922. He accepted a job on the La Porte Herald *in January of 1923.*

Will and Maria Pyle with Mary and George Bales in front of the Bales house, a mile west of the Pyle farm. They spent a lot of time together and would play a continuing role in the life of Ernie Pyle, "the roving reporter."

Starting as a cub reporter at the La Porte Herald *in La Porte, Indiana, for $25 per week, Ernie soon made his mark as a promising journalist. The city editor was Lee G. Miller, a Harvard graduate, who later became Ernie's managing editor at the Scripps-Howard newspaper syndicate in Washington, D.C.*

Ernie accepted a job with the Washington Daily News at $33 a week. Lee Miller had preceded Ernie by a month in joining the staff of the News. They became life-long friends.

Ernie learned to roll his own cigarettes, his trademark in later years, from his childhood mentor, Bill Bales.

While on the beat in Washington, Ernie was well known in aviation circles. He became known as the first reporter to research and write a national aviation column. He loved to fly. At one of their aviation dinners, Amelia Earhart presented him with a Hamilton wristwatch on behalf of all his flying buddies. He was the watch when he was killed in 1945, and it is now in the museum at the Ernie Pyle School of Journalism at Indiana University.

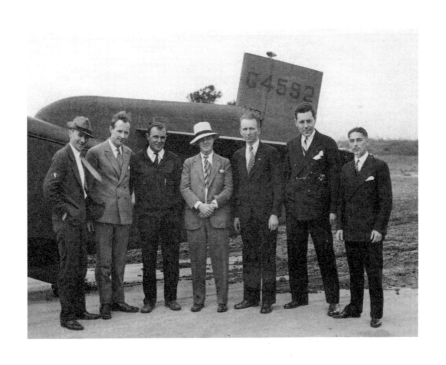

As a dashing Scripps-Howard reporter, he attracted much attention wherever he traveled. Here his father, Will Pyle, is bidding him farewell on his trip back to Washington on a TWA airline. Will Pyle would drive him to Indianapolis from Dana, a distance of 70 miles, to catch his plane.

During his years in Washington, he was constantly on the move and routinely took a DC-3 when he came back to visit his parents.

*During his tenure on the Washington Daily News he met a very attractive
girl from Minnesota who also was working in D.C. Ernie and Jerry got
separated in the shuffle of a crowd, but met again a year later. Smart,
beautiful, and elegant, Jerry became his wife and was always referred to in
his columns, as they traveled the U.S. together, as "that girl."*

Ernie and his father were very close, and were always competing to see who would weigh the most on the next visits. Their weights were usually somewhere around 120 pounds. This photo was taken on Main Street in Dana, Indiana, shortly after Will Pyle's car had jumped the curb and had crashed into the front window of the Rhoades Dry Goods Store. Will, it seems, had oiled his squeaking brakes, an event that was later retold in one of Ernie's columns.

The harsh environments of living with the combat troops and the constant burden of meeting his deadline for Scripps-Howard, took its toll on Ernie. He always was on the verge of pneumonia or a bad cold and smoked a lot. On his war correspondent's card he listed his weight as 115 pounds.

Upon his return from WW II, Ernie spent a few days at the Mound. He was tired, run-down, and had very little motivation to go on. He took his dad's rocking chair and a straight chair out in the front yard and sat in the September sun, absorbing thoughts and memories of bygone days.

Indiana University invited Ernie back to receive an honorary doctor's degree in letters. Ernie could not turn down Dean Edmondson. Here with Ernie are pals from college, Jack Hastings and Jim Adams. Today, the Indiana School of Journalism is named after him, containing a collection of personal memorabilia, including his typewriter and the Hamilton wristwatch presented to him by Amelia Earhart.

Ernie always had the greatest admiration for General Omar Bradley

31 January, 1945.

Dear Doctor,

May I extend my belated congratulations on the honor
recently bestowed on you by two universities. The honor was
well deserved and we were all very pleased to learn of the
awards. All of us over here miss you very much.

I hope that you were able to get a good rest and did
not push off to another theater until you had completely re-
covered your vim and vigor. Thank you very much for the
copy of your book, which I just received and have started to
read.

This winter has been a real trial on the soldiers in
the front line. We have had freezing weather continuously
for about seven weeks, and snow is now stacked up so that
in some places at the front we have two or three feet, with
drifts much deeper than this. A great consolation is that
the weather is just as hard or harder on the Boches as it
is on us.

As you know, we have just given the Germans a considerable beating in their attempt to break through our lines in
the Ardennes and their losses have been tremendous. I am
glad that we were able to inflict these losses before the
Russian offensive started so that they do not have these
fine divisions to throw against the Russians in an attempt
to stop their great offensive. We are continuing our attack
and hope that we can do a good job while the Russian offensive is going on.

If you do go to the Pacific area, be sure to take care
of yourself and your health, because we all want to see you
when this is over and we come back to the States.

The very best of luck to you.

Sincerely,

Brad

Mr. Ernie Pyle,
Albuquerque,
New Mexico.

During Ernie's visit to the Pacific, he stayed with his nephew, Jack Bales, a radar navigator on a B-29 crew that had flown 25 combat missions over Tokyo, flying out of Saipan. Ernie enjoyed having his own bunk for a change and his first association with a bomber crew. Captain Jack Bales is seated directly behind Ernie during a bull sessions This was just before the bomb was dropped on Hiroshima.

Will Pyle christens "The Ernie Pyle" a B-29 named in honor of his son, who only recently killed at Ie Shima.

Huge crowds attended the christening of the "The Ernie Pyle." It was christened by Will Pyle, in June of 1945 at Boeing's Wichita plant in Kansas.

Aircraft number 0118 bore the name of America's favorite war correspondent, Ernie Pyle. This was the only bomber ever to be named after a war correspondent. After being christened "The Ernie Pyle" it flew 7,000 miles to our air base at Saipan in the Marianas, where it was assigned to a B-29 wing under the command of General Curtis LeMay. Although armed and crewed for combat, this aircraft never flew a mission over Japan, because Colonel Paul Tibbets had just dropped the atomic bomb over Hiroshima, precipitating an end to the hostilities.

After the death of his son, Ernie, and the death of his wife, Maria, Will Pyle and his sister-in-law, "Aunt Mary," became ever more dependent upon family and friends. Will was going blind from cataracts and was generally in poor health. From left to right is Bill Bales, Aunt Mary Bales, Jack Bales, Beatrice Bales, who was Ernie's pen pal, Will Pyle, and the author, Bob Bales, taken in 1947.

About the Author

Bob Bales, the Pyle family historian, has lived a rich and colorful life. During WWII Bob flew B-24s, while his older brother, Jack, flew on B-29s. After the war, he flew out of the Philippines and covered most of the South Pacific. Ernie Pyle once wrote, "One day, Bob is going to go to Chicago to become a famous artist." After Korea, Bob worked for the Pentagon for over a decade. While stationed in the Pentagon (USAF) he organized and operated the Air Force Operational Art Program as the official illustrator to the Air Force. He invited professional artists from the Society of Illustrators in New York and L.A. to capture historical aviation events around the globe. After working a stint for Walt Disney on several major pictures, Bob played a key role on the 5-member team responsible for building Pepperdine's Malibu campus. Although he has a PhD in business administration, Bob still considers his greatest accomplishment to be reaching Eagle Scout status. "I am always interested in learning more about the natural world. There are only a few things more important than the responsible enjoyment and preservation of the great outdoors." He and his wife, Peggy, travel the world over from their home in Birmingham, Alabama. Bob is a retired Lieutenant Colonel in the regular Air Force.